Ghost Cat: Midnight Paws
Ghost Cat 2: Bid for Midnight

D1363683

Jessica Beck is the *New York Times* Bestselling Author of the Donut Mysteries, the Classic Diner Mystery Series, and the Ghost Cat Cozy Mysteries.

To absent friends

Chapter 1

"Trust me. You two are going to absolutely love this place," my mother said as she unlocked the temporary door to the old wagon factory she was having renovated. "I've been dying for you both to see it."

"Dot, do you have any idea how old this building is?" my husband, Jake, asked her as he idly stroked a brick wall near the entrance.

"As a matter of fact, I do. I've even ordered a plaque for the front of the building. It was built in 1889," she said proudly as she led the way inside. My mother had been insisting that we take this tour over a month since we'd gotten married, but just as we'd schedule it, something else would come up in her life to delay it. That was Momma, always busy with her latest project. I didn't know how she kept up with it all. As for me, my sole responsibility in life besides my husband was running my donut shop, and I loved it that way. Some folks might not have thought that it was challenging enough, but it was perfect for me. I was allowed enough creativity to develop new tasty treats for my customers, and yet most of my day-to-day life was the same. I'd get up before any person in their right mind was awake, make my way through the dark streets of April Springs, North Carolina to Donut Hearts, and start my day by making cake donuts first, and then yeast ones. Jake was growing restless, though. He'd been retired for less than two months from the state police, and I could tell all of that free time was beginning to wear on him.

"Amazing. Are you having any trouble finding materials to match the old structure?" he asked.

"More than I ever imagined I would. The windows were the absolute worst," she said. "I finally found a company in Germany that specializes in wavy glass. Aren't they perfect?"

"They're beautiful," Jake said as he admired the careful imperfections.

"It's going to be a real showplace when we're finished with it."

"It's going to be absolutely spectacular," I said as we walked farther into the building. The main space would ultimately be open, and sported a floor of stained antique hardwood clearly dating back to the building's origins. In the center of the room, the dark wood was broken up with the image of a lighter maple wagon wheel imbedded into the pattern, a circle of wooden pieces connected with spokes to a stone center, though it was now partially obscured by sheets of plastic hung down temporarily from the area above. There was no loft above that space, with only the heavy wooden timbers between the floor and the roof. The area was well lit even with no overhead lights on as skylights flooded the area with sunshine. Around the perimeter of the space, I could see a wooden stairway that wound itself upward to what appeared to be a series of smaller rooms upstairs. That must have been where the offices had originally been located.

On the first floor, I saw a hint of movement as a large sheet of plastic flickered in a nonexistent breeze. "Is anyone else here, Momma?"

"It wouldn't surprise me one bit. Workers are coming in and out of this place all of the time," Momma said just as we heard a door close on the other side of the building. "In fact, we must have just scared one off," she added with a grin.

Jake was keeping quiet, and when I glanced toward him, I saw that he was frowning. "What's wrong?"

"Something's not right. You both need to stay right here," he said solemnly as he pulled out a pistol I hadn't even known he'd been carrying. During his time as an investigator with the state police, Jake had been responsible for putting quite a few bad guys behind bars, and one of the downsides of that was that he'd never be able to rest easy without always having a way to protect himself from his past.

When Momma saw the gun in his hand, she frowned as well. "I'm sure it's nothing, Jake. Would you mind putting that thing away? It's making me nervous."

"Not just yet," my husband said softly. "You two keep talking like everything's normal. I need to check this out."

Clearly something had alerted him; I just couldn't imagine what might have done it. Still, I trusted his instincts, so I did exactly as he'd suggested. "Momma, what do you think of a new donut idea I've been playing with at the shop? I want to use mulled cider in the recipe."

"Wouldn't that be too powerful?" she asked as Jake moved slowly forward.

"Some of my customers seem to prefer flavors that reach up and grab them by the ears," I said as we watched Jake creep toward the still-moving plastic sheet. He was almost there, and it took everything I had not to hold my breath. Talking a little louder than I meant to, I asked, "Remember those Kool-Aid donuts I made awhile ago? They were strong enough to get up and walk away on their own, but they still had their fans."

"Well, they were certainly colorful enough," Momma said as Jake finally reached the plastic. Without a moment's hesitation, he stepped around the makeshift barrier near the center of the space, his gun leading the way, and I felt my heart suddenly stop.

"Call an ambulance," Jake called out a moment later.

I didn't even wait for further information as I pulled out my cellphone and hurried toward him. "What happened?" I asked as I dialed.

"Somebody stabbed this man in the chest with a piece of rebar," Jake said as he knelt down and searched for the victim's pulse.

I couldn't see who it was immediately because Jake was blocking my view of his face, but after I told the 911 dispatcher to send someone quickly, I knelt down beside my husband. I could finally see him clearly, and I recognized the man lying on the floor instantly. It was Sully Jackson, a local electrician, wearing one of his typical red-and-black-checked flannel shirts. He loved them so much that he insisted that his employees wear them as well as some kind of uniform, only this one was being stained by the man's blood. Sully never missed coming in on Saturday morning and buying a dozen donuts for his crew. As I looked a little more carefully, I saw the tip of the iron rod sticking out of his chest, and blood on his lips. It looked really bad as Sully's spilled blood began to creep across the wood-and-stone emblem embedded in the old factory floor beneath him.

"I'll meet the ambulance out front and bring them back here," Momma said as she headed to the front door.

"At least he's still breathing," my husband said as he stood after my mother was gone. "Stay with him, Suzanne."

"Where are you going?" I asked my husband as I looked down at Sully again.

"I'm going after whoever did this," Jake said.

I doubted Sully had much time left, not with the amount of blood that he'd clearly already lost. I reached out and took the electrician's right hand in mine, hoping to offer him any comfort that I could. "Just be careful," I called out to him, but either he didn't hear me, or he chose to ignore my request.

I didn't have time to worry about him, though. I had a dying man on my hands.

Sully squeezed my hand and tried to say something.

"Don't try to talk," I said as I knelt closer to his ear. "Hang in there, Sully. Help is on the way."

"It's important," Sully said, his voice a harsh, rasping whisper. As he spoke, a bubble of blood appeared on the corner of his mouth. It was clear that he was trying to tell me something, and just as crucial that I let him.

"What is it?" I asked as I leaned in even closer to his mouth. I could feel his hot breath on my ear as he squeezed my hand.

He gasped, and I had to wonder if another wave of pain had just shot through him. "Tried to steal from her." He wasn't making any sense, but I couldn't very well quiz him in his rapidly declining condition.

"Who did this to you, Sully? Who was trying to steal something? I need more information," I asked him, desperate to get anything that might help find the person who'd done this to him.

A chill suddenly went through me as I realized that his breath on my face had suddenly stopped.

"Sully? Can you hear me? Stay with me!" I pled as my voice got louder and louder.

But it was too late.

He was gone.

Chapter 2

The emergency medical techs tried their best, but it was clear that they were too late even as they continued to work on Sully's lifeless body. I felt a strong pair of arms envelop me, and I heard Jake whispering in my ear. "There was nothing any of us could do to help him. By the time we found him, it was already too late."

I knew that his words had been meant to comfort me, but they slid off me without any impact whatsoever. "Did you find who did this?" I asked him.

"Whoever did it was already gone," Jake said. "Suzanne, I never should have left you here alone with him. I'm sorry."

"Nonsense. You had to try to find the killer," I said.

"Did he say anything at all after I left?" Jake asked me softly.

I hated talking about it while the techs continued to work in vain, but Jake was right. This was important. "Just something that didn't make any sense. He must have been delirious."

"Tell me anyway," Jake ordered.

"He told me it was important, and then Sully said, 'Tried to steal from her.' I tried to get him to tell me who stabbed him, but by then it was too late."

"It's okay, Suzanne," Jake said as he continued to stroke my arms lightly, doing his best to comfort me.

"We both know full well that in no way is this okay," I said. "We have to figure this out."

"Let's see what Chief Grant has to say about it before we decide to do anything on our own," Jake told me.

"Stephen Grant is my friend, but we both know that he'll be in over his head on this," I said. "You have to get George to appoint you as a special investigator again." The mayor had done that once before, and I didn't see why he couldn't do it again. Jake had a lot more authority to investigate when he could say that he was working for the town of April Springs.

"I'm sorry, but I can't do that. He's already in enough trouble for doing it last time. I'm afraid that Grant's going to have to handle this on his own. If George appoints me again so soon after the last time, he's basically saying that Stephen isn't capable of running the police department on his own."

"Well, is he?" I asked him. "Don't get me wrong. I'm a big fan of the guy, but he's too young to have this kind of weight on him."

"I think he'll grow into it, if he's given a chance," Jake said earnestly.

"And what happens in the meantime? Does whoever did this to Sully go free because of his inexperience?"

"Don't worry, we won't let that happen," Jake said as he studied the crime scene.

As they were loading Sully up on the gurney and carting him away, I saw something fall off the stretcher and flutter to the floor. Without thinking, I reached down and retrieved it before it got lost in the chaos.

"What was that?" Jake asked me. "You shouldn't have touched it with your bare hands, Suzanne."

"If it had any prints on it at all, they were bound to be Sully's," I said as I studied the piece of paper in my hand. "It's the corner of a bill," I said.

"What, like an invoice?" Jake asked.

"No, it's money," I said as I offered it to him.

"You can't tell much about it, can you?" Jake asked as he pulled out his hanky and took the torn corner from me.

"We're not keeping it, are we?" I asked him.

"No, we'll turn it over to Grant as soon as he gets here," he said.

At that moment, the acting police chief, Stephen Grant, came into the warehouse, his face rigid and grim. "What happened?"

Jake proceeded to tell him, rattling off the facts as though he were some kind of robot. I knew that it was his training kicking in, but it never ceased to surprise me to see my husband go into full investigator mode. After he was finished, he handed the bill's corner to the chief.

"Are you sure that's exactly what he said, Suzanne?" Chief Grant asked me. "Take a second to think about it if you need to. It's important."

"Jake told you exactly what I heard. You knew Sully pretty well, didn't you?"

"I still do, Suzanne," Chief Grant said stubbornly. "They're still working on him, so as far as I'm concerned, he's not gone yet."

"I'm sorry. I didn't mean anything by it," I apologized quickly.

"I know you didn't," the interim chief said as he loosened up a bit. "Yeah, we were close. I worked for him as an unskilled helper over three summers when I was in high school. He was a good guy and the most honest man I'd ever met in my life. I can't believe someone would do this to him."

"I'm curious about that myself," Jake said. "What could anyone have against a harmless old man working as a subcontractor on this project?"

"You'd be surprised. The construction industry has its share of bad guys, though most of them are decent enough. Still, Sully banged heads with a few of them when I was around."

"What were their beefs with him?" Jake asked.

"Sully Jackson demanded only the best of everyone he came into contact with, because that's what he gave everything himself. I remember one time when he made me drive back to the hardware store in the middle of a job because the clerk had charged us twenty-five cents less than we owed him. I tried telling Sully that we could settle up after work, but he wouldn't have it. He lost more in my wages than he'd underpaid, but none of that mattered to him. Things had to be square for him."

"Don't worry; we'll figure out who did this," I said.

He looked at me askance for a moment before he spoke again. "Suzanne, does that mean you're going to meddle in this case?"

"I prefer to think of it as assisting around the edges of the official investigation," I said.

"I'm sure that you do," Chief Grant said, and then he turned to Jake. "How about you? Are you going to ask the mayor to make you a special investigator again? Normally I wouldn't mind it, but this time it's personal."

"George told me that after the last time, he couldn't do that again," Jake said. "Short of joining your force, I'm just another civilian, no different from anyone else."

"I'd never say that," Chief Grant said. "Does that mean that you'll be helping her, now that Grace is out of the picture?"

My best friend, Grace Gauge, was his girlfriend, so of course he'd heard about her decision to retire from our amateur sleuthing, but still, it hurt a little hearing him say it. "I'm not entirely convinced that she's really retired," I said.

"Trust me. She's finished," Chief Grant said. "So, I asked you a question, Jake. Are you going to dig into this, too?"

"Would that necessarily be a bad thing if I did?" he asked the acting police chief.

For a moment, there was tense silence that felt as though it were dragging on forever. Finally, Chief Grant spoke. "Officially, you understand that I can't condone anything you or your wife might do," he said overbearingly before he added with a grin, "but I can't exactly stop you, either. All I ask is that you keep me in the loop on everything you uncover."

"We can do that," Jake said, but Chief Grant wasn't finished yet.

"Jake, I know that you are used to taking the lead on the murder cases you've investigated in the past, but you have to let me do my job on this one. That means that the official channels are all mine. Are we clear on that? You may be more qualified to hold this job than I am, but until you replace me, I'm going to be the one running the show."

"I wouldn't have it any other way," Jake said as he took the chief's hand and shook it firmly.

"Good. I'm glad we're clear on that. Now, did you get a good look at whoever might have done this to Sully?"

"Not even a glimpse," Jake admitted. "By the time I got outside, whoever had been there was gone."

The chief was about to speak when three of his officers entered the building together. Grant spoke to us softly before addressing his staff. "We'll talk later." Then he turned to his officers. "We need to seal off this building, as well as the alley in back. Understood?"

As they went to work with their official investigation, Jake took me by the arm and gently led me back out the front door. Momma was still standing there, clearly distraught about what had just happened.

"I can't believe this is happening," she said. "I was just speaking with Sully this morning."

"Did he say anything that might be related to what happened to him?" Jake asked her.

"No! We talked about the weather, if you can imagine that."

Jake offered her some comfort, and then he said, "Let's go back to the cottage where we can all deal with this on more familiar ground."

"Yes. That's a fine idea," Momma said. She'd driven us to the building, so we all piled into her car and headed back to the place the two of us had once shared.

"There's something I need to do. Momma, could you drop me off at Grace's along the way?" I asked her.

Jake looked at me carefully before he spoke. "Suzanne, you heard the chief. Grace is officially retired."

"I know she keeps saying it, but I've got to at least ask her if she wants to help. You can see that, can't you?"

"Just don't be too disappointed if she turns you down," Jake replied.

"I won't," I said, though I wasn't entirely sure that was

true. Grace and I had dug into more murders than I cared to remember, and there had never been a time when she'd turned down my request for help.

That had been before we'd nearly died during our last investigation, though.

Even as well as I knew her, I still wasn't sure if she'd meant it when she'd told me that she was finished investigating murder with me.

There was only one way to find out for sure, and that was to ask her directly myself.

Chapter 3

"Grace, open up! It's me. I see your car in the driveway!" I'd been knocking for the past full minute, but my best friend was not answering my summons. Did she honestly believe that I'd just give up and go away? The front door finally opened, and Grace stepped aside to invite me in. She was in her robe, and she was drying her hair with a towel. "Hey, Suzanne. I was in the shower. How long have you been standing out there knocking? What's going on?"

"Have you heard the news yet?" I asked as I walked into her house. On the surface, Grace was everything I was not; she was slim and beautiful, while I was more than a couple of pounds overweight, and though I'd been called cute plenty of times in my life, no one but Jake had ever called me beautiful. None of that mattered, though. We were sisters from different mothers, and had been for practically all of our lives.

"What news are you talking about?" she asked. "It must be serious."

"How do you know that?"

She grinned at me. "Because you aren't giving me a hard time about taking a shower in the middle of the afternoon."

"Why would I tease you about that? I take them myself just about every day," I said.

"That's because you'll smell like donuts if you don't. My explanation is much less logical. I just felt like it, so I took one. That's one of the great things about being a grown-up. I can have dessert for dinner and pretty much do as I please when it comes to everything else."

I laughed. "When's the last time you had your treat before you ate your meal?"

"Okay, it's been awhile, but I could if I wanted to," she said. "Come on back into the bedroom. I'll get dressed while you tell me all about the big news." She hesitated a moment, and then she grinned at me. "You're not pregnant, are you?"

I shook my head. "It's bad enough that Momma wants to rush things, but you, too? I haven't even been married for very long, and folks are already asking me if I'm going to have a baby soon."

"Well, we both know that you're not getting any younger," she said with a grin as we walked back into her bedroom. I took a seat on the bed while she disappeared into her master closet. It was bigger than my bedroom back at the cottage, but it still barely managed to hold all of Grace's clothes. She needed most of them for her job as a cosmetics sales rep, but even her casual attire was nicer than my best outfit.

"Need I remind you that we're the same age?" I asked her.

"Maybe so, but I'm not the one who just got married," she said as she poked her head out of her closet for a brief moment. "If that's not the big news, then what is?"

Grace had just vanished again when I told her, "Sully Jackson was murdered this afternoon."

"What happened?" Grace asked as she poked her head out of the closet again.

"Momma was showing off the remodeling job they're doing on the old wagon factory to Jake and me, and we stumbled over him right after someone stabbed him with a small length of rebar."

"That's terrible," she said as she disappeared again. "Did you see who killed him?"

"No, he managed to escape. Jake chased him outside, but he somehow managed to get away." Grace suddenly appeared, now dressed in stylish slacks and a cute top, looking as though she'd just stepped out of a high-end catalogue.

"Tell me something; is it hard always looking that good?"

She laughed. "Please. There's nothing easy about it. It's a shame about Sully. You two were friends, weren't you? Didn't he come by the donut shop?"

"You know me. I get attached to my customers," I said.
"So, I was wondering–"
"No."
"Hang on a second. You didn't even let me finish asking the question," I said.
"I don't need to hear the rest of it to know what my answer is going to be. Suzanne, I meant what I said. I've officially retired from amateur sleuthing."

We'd had a close call not that long ago, and in the heat of the moment, Grace had told me that she was finished investigating crime with me. I'd hoped that once she had time to mull it over, she'd change her mind, but if that was going to be the case, evidently enough time hadn't passed yet. "How can you just stop?" I asked her. "Isn't it in your blood, too?"

"Suzanne, I'm not about to deny that I enjoyed digging into a few local murder investigations with you, but that last time was just too much for me to take. We could have died out in that forest."

"But we didn't," I said. "We outsmarted the killer, remember?"

"We got lucky, and you know it," she said.

"I'm not denying it, but luck's a part of life. The important thing is that we walked away from it unscathed."

"No, the important thing is that I'm not going to press my luck ever again, and neither should you."

"Grace, I can't just walk away. Sully meant something to me, and besides, it happened in my momma's building. That makes me doubly involved."

"Maybe you should talk to Jake about it," she said.
"Suzanne, I'm not entirely unsympathetic to your motivation, but it doesn't affect me. If you think about it, most of the murders we investigated in the past were because of your ties, not mine. I'm sorry, but I just can't bring myself to do it anymore."

I could see that Grace was deadly earnest in her refusal to help me. It was time to drop it.

I hugged her for a moment, and then I pulled away.

"What was that for?" she asked me.

"For everything you've done in the past to help me on my cases," I said. "Don't worry; I won't ask you again."

Grace looked at me tentatively for a moment before she spoke again. "Hey, are we okay?"

"We're golden," I said with a smile. "There are lots of things we can do together besides tracking down killers."

"Like lunch. Or even dinner. Shopping is fun, too."

I laughed. "You're good for my soul, Grace."

"We could go do something right now, if you'd like," she suggested. "I'm free for the rest of the day."

"Unfortunately, I'm not."

"At least tell me that Jake is going to work with you investigating the case," Grace said. "If something ever happened to you because I refused to help you out, I'd never be able to forgive myself."

I looked at her solemnly for a moment, and then I said, "You are officially absolved of any consequences that might come my way due to my investigation from here on out. How's that?"

"You never answered my question, though I've brought it up a few times now. Is Jake going to work with you?"

I shrugged. "I'm not entirely sure what the pecking order is regarding who is working for whom, but yes, we're working together."

"Then you don't even need me, do you?" she asked with a broad grin.

"I never said that," I answered, smiling in turn. "And I won't, not in a million years."

"Thanks for understanding," Grace said as we walked out of the bedroom toward her front door.

"Always and forever," I said. "We'll grab something to eat soon. I promise."

"We'd better," she said as I left her.

As I walked the short stretch of road that separated our homes, it finally started to sink in. A part of me had believed that once Grace was presented with another local murder, she'd forget all about her promise to retire and dive right into it with me again.

It seemed that wasn't going to happen, though.

At least she was right about one thing.

I still had Jake as a partner, and he was more than qualified for the job.

While I'd been inside Grace's home trying to convince her to help me again, I realized that things had been happening at the cottage. My Jeep was parked in the driveway where I'd left it, along with Jake's old decrepit truck, but those weren't the only two vehicles there.

Momma's stylish car was still there as well.

It appeared that we were about to have our very own war council.

"What's up?" I asked as I walked in, taking my jacket off and hanging it in the closet. To my surprise, Momma wasn't the only visitor we had; her husband, the former chief of police, was there as well. "Hi, Phillip," I said, the name still perched awkwardly on my tongue. He'd been Chief Martin for as long as I'd known him, but ever since he'd retired—and not coincidentally become my stepfather—I'd been forced to call him by his given name. Momma must have dashed home, collected him, and then returned to the cottage, all in less time than I'd taken to speak with Grace.

"Hello, Suzanne," he said from his seat by the fireplace. "How's Grace?"

"Standing firm," I said a little sadly, and then I turned to Jake. "She's not going to change her mind. I'm sorry, but it's just going to be the two of us."

"We'll be fine," Jake said. "As a matter of fact, I've been trying to talk Phillip into joining our little team."

He *what*? I would have at least liked to have had the chance to talk my husband out of it in private beforehand, but I was stuck now. What was Jake thinking? While it was true that Phillip had been a good police chief, we were still trying to

find a way to be in the same room together, let alone work on
a case side by side.

My stepfather said with a wry grin, "Don't worry, Suzanne.
I turned him down."

"As was your right," Momma said. "Phillip, you retired
from being a police officer for a reason."

"So did Jake," I said, defending him, even though I wanted
to strangle him at that moment.

"Yes, but Jake is quite a bit younger than my husband is,"
Momma said.

"Hang on a second. I'm not *that* old," the former chief
protested. "If I wanted to, I know that I could be a valuable
asset in their investigation."

"That's just what Stephen Grant needs on his plate," I said.
"Momma, if Phillip's joining, why don't you come on board,
too?" As soon as the words were out of my mouth, I knew
that I'd made a mistake. Jake looked at me sharply, which
meant that my offer was another conversation we'd have to
be having soon. Maybe that was how he'd ended up inviting
Phillip to join our investigation. If it was, I'd have to cut him
some slack.

"No, thank you," Momma said. "Phillip and I are quite
happy in retirement."

"You can say that because I'm the only one who actually
retired," he said to my mother. Wow, I had to give the man
credit. He had guts saying that the way he did.

I braced myself for the fiery retort from my mother, and
then I heard her say softly, "I'm sorry. I keep trying to cut
back on my workload, but there are too many opportunities
everywhere for me to turn them all down."

Did my mother just apologize to her husband in front of us?
It wasn't entirely unprecedented for her to say that she was
sorry, but it still happened infrequently enough to make it
noteworthy.

Before I could take that in, Momma followed up by saying,
"You could always do something with me in real estate.
Your skills would come in handy, I assure you."

"What skills are those?" Phillip asked her.

"I shouldn't have to remind you that you ran an entire police department, so that means you can handle personnel, budgets, and all sorts of problems that come up. That would make you perfect for what I do as well."

"You know me. I'm just not the mogul type," Phillip said with a grin. "Besides, I've been really enjoying digging into April Springs' local history. That's where you got all of that information on the old wagon factory, remember? I have plenty to do on my own, and no desire to help you run your little empire."

"That's not what I meant, and you know it."

I was suddenly seeing more of my mother's married life than I wanted to. "Maybe you two should continue this discussion at home," I suggested.

Momma grinned at me, but there wasn't a great deal of joy in it. "Are you asking us to leave, Suzanne?"

"No, of course not," I said, and then I turned to Jake. "Grab your coat."

"Where are you two going?" Momma asked sharply.

"Well, you two clearly need some privacy, so if you're determined to stay here, Jake and I are going to take a walk." I turned to him and asked, "Right?"

"Whatever you say," Jake said. He grabbed both of our jackets, and I knew that my mother and her husband weren't the only ones who needed some time to talk.

"This is utter nonsense," Momma said. "Phillip, let's go."

"Fine," her husband said as he stood. "I'm not sure what good it's going to do to have this particular conversation again, though. We've already talked the topic to death."

"Perhaps, but we haven't resolved it yet, so there clearly needs to be more discussion."

Phillip offered Jake a gentle grin as he walked toward the door, acting as though they shared something in common. As a matter of fact, they did, something besides being married to a mother and her daughter. They'd both chosen to wed strong-willed women, and that meant that sometimes there would be days like these. In the end, I hoped that they both found their experiences worthwhile overall.

"We'll talk again soon," Momma said to me as they started out the door.

"You can count on it," I said as I leaned forward and hugged her goodbye.

After they were gone, I turned to Jake and grinned. "So, is it a wash? We're even, wouldn't you say?"

"Suzanne, what are you talking about?"

"I asked Momma to join us without thinking, and I'm assuming that you made the invitation to Phillip the same way. Let's call it even and forget it ever happened."

Jake thought about it for a few moments, and then he nodded in agreement. "Done and done. So, Grace is out?"

"I'm afraid so. It looks as though you're stuck with me as an investigative partner. That is, unless you've changed your mind and you've decided to ask George for official status despite what you said earlier."

"Like I said, that's not going to happen. I'm afraid that we're just going to have to get by on our wits this time."

"Don't be so depressed about it," I said after I kissed his cheek lightly. "After a while you get used to not having any official status."

"So, all we are is a pair of nosy busybodies, then," Jake said.

"We're a great deal more than that. Think of us as independent contractors. We're not officially on anyone's payroll, so nobody can fire us."

"There's always that," Jake said with a grin. "Okay, I'll bite. Where do we start? I'm new to conducting an investigation from this perspective."

"No worries, because you have an excellent partner who's done it a dozen times before," I said with a grin. "The first thing we need to do is to tap into the underground network that's not readily available to the police."

"What network is that?" Jake asked.

"I need to speak with Gabby Williams."

"You mean 'we,' don't you?"

"Jake, she's not going to speak freely in front of you, and besides, there's no danger in me approaching her alone. Gabby's not dangerous." I thought about that, and then quickly corrected myself. "Not that way, anyway."

"In what way is she threatening, exactly?" Jake asked, clearly concerned by my assessment.

"She can kill a reputation like that," I said as I snapped my fingers.

"Is that all?" Jake asked, relieved by my response.

"Trust me, it's not nothing," I said.

"Suzanne, how exactly is Gabby going to be able to help us? Was she sleeping with Sully or something?"

The mere thought of it shocked me, though I wouldn't put it past the woman. "I don't think so, but you never know."

"Then why should we approach her first?" Jake asked. "If you ask me, we should go straight to the source. Let's start with Sully's employees."

"You're still thinking too much like a cop," I said. "Chief Grant has already spoken with them both, unless I miss my guess. We'll tackle them tomorrow after we're certain that he's finished with them, but we have to stay out on the edges, remember?"

"And Gabby is the best source in town that you have?" Jake asked me, still not believing it.

"Believe me, she knows every bit of dirt in town. If there's something we can learn about Sully, she's the one to approach."

"And she's just going to give you this information freely?" Jake asked me.

"Well, it might take a little finesse, but remember, I've dealt with her before, and that means that I have to do it solo. Do you honestly mind if I approach her by myself?"

"I don't suppose so," Jake said, even though it was clear from his tone of voice that he minded very much indeed.

"Don't worry. It's all going to work out fine. I won't be

long," I said as I kissed him, and then I grabbed my coat. I needed to get out of there as soon as possible. I knew that the longer I stayed, the harder Jake would try to talk me out of approaching Gabby without him. It wasn't that he considered her a danger; he just hated being out of the loop, and I could hardly blame him.

There were just some things that I had to do on my own, and this was definitely one of them.

Chapter 4

"I was wondering when I'd see you," Gabby Williams said as I walked into her gently used clothes shop, ReNEWed. It was just down the road from Donut Hearts, a fact that brought us into contact every now and then, but not as often as some folks might think. Gabby had her circle of friends, and I had mine, and they barely overlapped at all. However, we had a tenuous relationship that I planned to exploit.

"Am I that predictable?" I asked as I took off my jacket. Jumping right into my motivation for being there wasn't a great idea. I knew from experience that the longer it took me to bring up my questions, the fewer hoops I would have to jump through to get my answers. As I let my hand linger on a nearby blouse, I asked, "Anything new in?"

"Suzanne, the entire point of my shop is that *none* of it is new," she said disdainfully, studying me as she spoke. Gabby was a trim woman in her fifties, always dressed stylishly in only the best apparel her shop received. Her eyes were red, and I had to wonder if her allergies were bothering her. It was certainly the right time of the year for them.

"You know what I mean," I said as I searched the closest racks of clothing.

"Sorry, but we don't have anything in your size or your taste," she said a little harshly. I might have taken offense at the crack from some folks, but I knew that Gabby was just being Gabby. "Besides, I didn't think you'd be coming around for clothing, not given what just happened."

"What's that?" I asked her, pretending to be uninterested.

"Suzanne Hart, you stumbled upon a man's body not two hours ago, and then you try to come waltzing in here as though nothing happened."

"You're talking about Sully Jackson, aren't you?" I asked. Not surprisingly, the news had evidently traveled fast in our small town.

Gabby raised an eyebrow in my direction critically. "That depends. Did you happen to find any *other* dead bodies since you found his?"

"No, just the one," I said as nonchalantly as I could manage. "It's tragic, but it's not any concern of mine. The police are handling it."

Gabby scoffed. "You aren't talking about young Officer Grant, are you? He's barely capable of handing out a parking ticket, let alone solving a murder."

"I don't know what you're talking about. Stephen Grant is turning out to be a very competent chief of police, and we're lucky to have him," I said. It was all I could do to hide my interest in the topic, but if I gave Gabby the upper hand, I'd be there all afternoon before she agreed to help.

"The jury's still out on him, if you ask me. I've been curious about something. Why didn't your husband want the job? Goodness knows that he's more than qualified enough for it."

"He's retired, Gabby. Do you have something like this in red?"

"I don't, but even if I did, it wouldn't work with your skin tones," she said dismissively. "Are you telling me that you and Grace aren't even going to investigate what happened to Sully?" Gabby seemed clearly disappointed by my reaction to the murder, which was curious.

"Grace has officially retired as my investigative partner," I explained, amazed that it stung a little to admit it so openly.

Gabby took that in for a moment before she spoke again. "That's a shame, but it's perfectly understandable. After all, how many times can you put yourself directly in the line of danger and not have it impact your life?"

"Apparently more times than I've experienced yet," I said.

"So, you *are* investigating," Gabby said triumphantly, as though she'd won a point in a debate, which was really all that every conversation with her ever was.

It was time to give her a little nudge. "I don't know. The truth is that I wouldn't know where to start. Sully was such a private person."

"To some folks," Gabby said almost wistfully. I glanced over at her and saw that she was frowning slightly. Apparently my instincts to come there first had been dead on the money.

"Are you implying that you knew him better than I did?" I asked her.

"I know lots of folks in April Springs," she said, suddenly deflecting my attention.

I wasn't going to let her, though. "I get it, Gabby, you're in the loop. Don't forget, I know a lot of folks around town, too." Waving my hand in the air dismissively, I said, "Thanks for your time. I'll try again in a few weeks. Maybe you'll get something in that works for me by then."

I was two steps away from the door and beginning to regret my bluff of leaving when Gabby said, "Things are kind of slow at the moment. Would you care for a cup of tea?"

"Why not?" I asked, doing my best not to reveal how eager I was to get her opinion about who might have wanted to murder Sully Jackson.

Gabby surprised me by walking toward the front door and flipping her sign to show that she was closed.

"I don't want you to lose any business on my account," I said.

"Nonsense. Turning them away every now and then just makes them want what I have more. You could take a lesson there yourself. Now that you're married, how long are you going to continue to keep your shop open seven days a week?"

"It's taxing at times, but what day should I close? It can't be on the weekend; I have too many standing orders then. What day of the workweek could I shut the shop down? Each day brings its own unique set of customers."

"So, let them change their routines. I have an idea. Why don't you close on Wednesdays? Remember the old days when everything closed on Wednesday afternoon around here? You could take the entire day off and spend it with your new husband."

"I'll think about it," I said. "But I've already shaved a few hours off each workday, and you wouldn't believe how some folks are still howling about that."

"Let them complain," she said with a shrug. "It's good for them. Now, let's see about that tea."

We walked to the back of the store together and into Gabby's office. The space was quite a bit nicer than the former cubbyhole of a closet I'd converted into my office at the donut shop, but then again, Gabby had a great deal more square footage than I had to work with. After all, I was reminded daily that Donut Hearts had been converted from a tiny old train depot, and it didn't leave me a great deal of space to work with.

As the teapot started to whistle, Gabby said, "I'm really going to miss Sully."

The tenderness of her admission surprised me. "Were you two really that close?" I asked her.

"As a matter of fact, I was quite fond of him," she said, avoiding giving me a direct answer. "Though I might have been in the minority of the people around him."

That news was interesting. "I've heard so many people describe Sully as the last genuinely honest man left on the planet that it's hard for me to imagine anyone wishing him harm."

"Don't you see that's what threw some folks off?" Gabby asked as she prepared the tea. "In fact, I'm willing to bet that's why he was murdered. Sully took his integrity to the limits, and some folks considered it a handicap more than a virtue."

"Who thought that?" I asked her.

"Well, right off the bat, I can think of a few folks. His two employees come to mind."

"Who worked for him in his electrical contracting business?" I asked.

"Bob Greene and Jim Burr. Sully often said that if he didn't keep an eye on the two of them, they'd walk out with his kitchen sink."

"That doesn't make any sense. If he didn't trust them, why did he hire them in the first place?" I asked as Gabby delivered an elegant china coffee cup to me, brimming with freshly brewed tea.

"What choice did he have? If he waited for someone with the level of honesty he had, he said that he'd have to work alone for the rest of his life, and he was beginning to feel the aches and pains he'd earned from a lifetime of physical labor."

I made a mental note to talk to Bob Greene and Jim Burr at my earliest opportunity, but there had to be more than two names on Gabby's mind. Unfortunately, the only way I was going to get any more information out of her was by threatening to walk away. I took a sip of tea, nodded, and then returned my cup to its saucer as I stood. "Thanks for the tea and the information," I said as I headed back toward the front of the shop.

"Sit back down, Suzanne. We haven't even begun to scratch the surface yet," Gabby ordered.

It was a command that I had no problem obeying. "Do you mean there's more?"

"Oh, yes. I'm willing to bet that you wouldn't have considered Carl Descent."

The name surprised me, but I tried not to show it. "Why would Carl want to kill Sully?"

"He tried to buy the building when it came up for sale, but your mother scooped it up with a last-second offer."

"I still don't understand what that had to do with Sully."

"Evidently Descent wanted to take the building down to the ground, brick by brick, and it offended Sully to think that a piece of our history was going to be destroyed. He put in a good word for her with the former owner, and that was one of the main reasons the man chose to sell the place to your mother instead of the developer. Weren't you aware of any of that?"

"I'm the first to admit that I don't know much about my

mother's business," I conceded. "You're not implying that she did anything wrong, are you?"

"Heavens, no," Gabby said quickly. She knew that even she couldn't get away with saying anything disparaging about my mother in front of me. Momma and I had our fair share of squabbles, but no one was allowed to say one bad word about her as far as I was concerned, and I knew that she felt the same way about me. "It was all perfectly legal and aboveboard. Besides Sully's recommendation, the owner wanted a parcel of land your mother owned, so she included it in her offer. Even though it seemed as though her bid wasn't the highest, it was the one the seller took. That aggravated Carl to no end, and he vowed to stop the project, no matter what it took."

"Even murder?" I asked incredulously. "That's hard to believe."

Gabby just shrugged. "I wouldn't put it past him. The man's unbalanced, if you ask me." Almost as an afterthought, she added, "The building is haunted, you know."

"I've heard the stories about strange lights there at night and odd noises coming from upstairs like everyone else in town has," I admitted. "You don't believe that there are actually ghosts inhabiting the place, do you?"

"Don't be so quick to scoff, Suzanne," Gabby said. "There are more things happening in our world that defy explanation than you can imagine."

"So, do you think that ghosts had something to do with Sully's murder?"

"I'm just saying that it might not be a bad idea to keep an open mind," Gabby said. This was getting strange, even for a conversation with Gabby, and that was saying something.

"Let's put a pin in that, shall we? Are there any other folks who might make your list?"

Gabby frowned, and then she answered, "Well, Shirley Edam has to be on your list."

"Shirley? Why her?" I asked. Shirley was no stranger to

my donut shop, and she'd always seemed nice to me in the past.

"She's his only competitor in town. Who are folks going to call now when they need electrical work done? Shirley's business just doubled."

"It's not enough reason to commit murder," I said, having a hard time believing that it was possible.

"Maybe so, if that were the extent of it, but there were other reasons as well," Gabby said.

"I'm listening," I said when more facts were not forthcoming.

"The two of them dated once upon a time," Gabby replied, clearly finding the admission distasteful.

"Seriously? When?"

"It was a few months ago, but she wasn't happy that it ended. Lately they started discussing the possibility of going into business together, and evidently Shirley thought that Sully was more interested in a personal merger, if you know what I mean."

It wasn't that hard to figure it out, given her broad hinting. "So, what happened?"

"Sully set her straight that this was strictly a business proposal, and she was furious! Granted, he didn't handle the situation very well, but Shirley really overreacted."

A suspicion was gnawing at the corner of my mind, so I carefully framed my next question. "You two have been dating lately, haven't you?"

Gabby actually blushed, and I knew that I'd hit home. "Suzanne Hart, what in the world ever gave you that idea?"

"You did," I said. "Why the big secret, though? Neither one of you were married."

"No, but at our ages, we decided to see how things worked out quietly before we announced our intentions to the world." Gabby appeared as though she were about to cry as she added, "We never got the chance to do that, though."

"I'm so sorry for your loss," I said, patting her shoulder awkwardly. That explained a great deal. If she were indeed in a relationship with Sully, it made sense that he'd confide in her. Without realizing it, I had indeed tapped into the best source of information in April Springs that I could have found. There was one thing left to do, and I knew that it wasn't going to be very popular with her. "Gabby, you need to tell Chief Grant everything that you just told me."

She looked shocked by my suggestion. "What are you talking about, Suzanne?"

"He needs this information if he's going to solve Sully's murder," I said. "Without it, he's working in the dark."

"You should tell him," Gabby said gruffly as she turned away.

"I would if I could, but he needs to hear this from you, and soon."

Gabby looked at me with a look of bewilderment. "I thought you said that you were going to investigate his murder yourself?"

It was time to come clean with her, but I might be able to use her ignorance to my advantage. "I will, but on one condition."

"That I tell Grant what I know," she said woodenly. "If I do that, do you promise that you'll dig into Sully's murder?"

"If you come clean with the police chief about everything you know, I'll even see if I can get Jake to help me do it," I said.

"Sold," she said quickly. "I'm holding you to this, Suzanne."

"I give you my word," I said, doing my best not to show the slightest hint of a smile. I'd just promised her to do something that I'd already planned to do in exchange for her doing something I knew she'd never have done otherwise.

"Then we both need to go," Gabby said as she gathered up our cups and the teapot.

"Where are we going?" I asked her, startled by the suddenness of her actions.

"I'm going to find Chief Grant, and you're going to go recruit your husband."

"I can do that," I said.

We parted ways outside, Gabby going to her car and me heading back to the cottage on foot. It was time to bring Jake up to speed on everything I'd just learned. I'd been hoping for a bit of useful information from Gabby, and instead, I'd gotten an avalanche of it.

Now we just had to sort out our suspects and see who had the opportunity to kill Sully Jackson.

At least we had a pretty solid grasp on when the murder had taken place. The time of death was usually not so specific, but we'd been on the site just after the fatal attack, so we had that going for us, which was something we couldn't always count on.

That fact, plus the information Gabby had provided about likely suspects, might mean that we'd be able to wrap this case up quickly.

I wasn't holding my breath, though.

It had been my experience that nothing was ever that easy, and in the end, it turned out that I was right on the money this time as well.

Chapter 5

When I got back to the cottage, I was surprised to find Jake sitting out on the front porch, swinging impatiently as he stared back toward the park. "Hey. What's up?" I asked him as I approached.

He jumped off the swing as though he were sitting on a spring. "What took you so long? I was about ready to come after you."

"Jake, I warned you that it might take some time to get Gabby to open up. I was kind of surprised how well it went, myself."

"Did you have any luck getting any information out of her, or do we need to start our investigation from scratch?"

"I'll tell you all about it, but let's go inside so I can warm up my hands. I know that the calendar says that it's officially spring, but I didn't wear a heavy enough jacket for the walk."

"Would you rather warm your hands up with the truck heater, instead?" he asked. "It blasts better heat than you'll get inside without the fireplace going."

Not many things worked well on Jake's ancient truck, but the heater it sported was still first rate. "Are you that eager to get started?" I asked him with a grin.

"You would be too, if you'd been sitting here waiting."

He had a point. "Okay. You drive while I warm up my hands."

My husband looked surprised by the speed of my agreement, but he was too smart to question it. Jake jogged around and opened my door for me, something that I didn't think I'd ever tire of. "Where do we go first?" he asked.

"Well, it's going to take a few minutes before I can tell you everything so we can come up with a plan. We could always park at the donut shop and chat there."

"No, that might give some folks the mistaken impression that you're open for business. Why don't we go to the crime scene and chat there?"

"You want to go back to the wagon factory?" I asked him.

"Call it whatever you'd like, but you knew what I meant."

"I suppose it's as good a place as any," I said as the heater kicked out enough warmth to cook a roast. My hands had gone past getting warm and were now starting to roast in the oppressive heat. "Could you turn that down a notch?"

Jake grinned at me as he did as I'd requested. "I told you it was a good heater."

"I never doubted it for an instant," I said as Jake drove past Grace's place. Her company car was gone, and I wondered where she was off to. One thing I was fairly certain of was that she wasn't investigating any murders. It appeared that part of her life was over, at least for the foreseeable future. Whether she'd ever come back to it was anyone's guess, but I knew from our recent conversation that it wouldn't be any time soon. We drove past the donut shop, through the center of town, and then onto the road toward Union Square, though we didn't have to go anywhere that far. Just on the edge of town limits, Jake pulled into the parking lot of the old wagon factory.

We weren't the only ones there, though.

A police squad car was parked in front of the building, and one of the police chief's officers was out front, apparently standing guard.

Jake pulled in, and the officer walked over to us before he could shut the truck engine off.

"Sorry, folks, but the building's closed," the man said solemnly, and then he grinned at us both as he added, "My orders were to let you down easy if you came asking."

"Thanks, Griffin," Jake said cordially. "I appreciate that."

"You don't have any donuts on you, do you, Suzanne?" the officer asked me.

Though he hadn't been in town—or on the force, for that matter—very long, Happy Griffin was another cop/customer of mine, so all of us knew each other.

"Come by tomorrow morning and I'll take care of you, on the house," I said with a smile.

"I appreciate the offer, but the chief won't let us take anything we don't pay for," Griffin said. "Sorry I can't let you in."

"We understand completely," Jake said. "Do you mind if we park over there and just look at the building, as long as we stay in the truck?"

"You can have a picnic for all I care," he said, and then he went back to his station. He'd been a fairly new hire, and Stephen Grant was the only chief he'd ever known. Though he hadn't been in town long, Griffin was a welcome addition as far as I was concerned. Anyone who liked donuts as much as he did was okay in my book, until I learned something that made me think otherwise.

"So, tell me what you've got," Jake said after he'd backed the truck up in a parking space so we could see the building without turning our heads.

"Don't you feel funny just sitting here like this?" I asked him. Griffin was doing his best to ignore us, but we'd made eye contact a few times, and when we did, he offered me a three-finger salute and grinned.

"The view might spark something," Jake said, "but if you really want to go, we can find somewhere else to park."

"No, this is fine," I said, doing my best to ignore the new patrolman.

"What did Gabby have to say?" he asked.

"Sully didn't trust the two guys working for him, Bob Greene and Jim Burr. Evidently there was some bad blood between them. She also said that one potential suspect is Carl Descent. He's been trying to get the project shut down since before it even started. Apparently Momma outbid him at the last second, and he's been mad ever since. What brings Sully into the mix is that he found out Descent was going to raze the building, so he put in a good word for Momma with the owner."

"Wow, that's a lot to digest in one session," Jake said.

"Hang on. There's more. Sully also managed to alienate his competitor, a woman who thought they were discussing more than merging their electrical contractor operations. Her name is Shirley Edam, and it sounds as though she had a few reasons of her own to want to make Sully suffer."

"How in the world did Gabby gather that much information so quickly? Sully just died a few hours ago."

"It turns out that she had the inside track. She was dating the man," I said.

"Wow. That puts an entirely different spin on things, doesn't it?"

"Jake, you don't think for one minute that Gabby had anything to do with Sully's murder, do you? Take it from me. She didn't do it."

"Suzanne, I know that she's a friend of yours, but how can you be so sure?" Jake asked me carefully.

"Because I know Gabby," I said.

Jake thought about that for a few seconds, and then he asked, "Would you mind if she at least stays on my list until I get my own reasons to take her off?"

"That's fine, but you should know that she's not even going on mine," I said.

"Agreed. We've certainly got a lot to work with. That was smart going to Gabby for information, Suzanne."

I loved hearing his praise, but I couldn't take credit for all of it. "To be perfectly honest, I had no idea that they were dating, Jake."

"I understand that, but you still knew the best source to tap in April Springs, and you went after the information. The fact that Gabby knew so much was just icing on the cake. You're better at this than some folks around town give you credit for."

"Do you mean you?" I asked him with a smile.

"Not me. I've always known you had the knack."

I laughed out loud at his comment. "I know better. It took you a long time to come on board, and you know it."

"What can I say? You convinced me," he replied as he started the truck.

"Where are we going?" I asked him as I waved good-bye to Griffin.

"We need to tell Chief Grant everything you just learned."

"It's already been taken care of," I said. "Gabby was on her way to see him when I left her."

Jake looked surprised by the news. "Was that her idea, or yours?"

"We made a deal. You and I would investigate the murder, but only if she told the chief everything she knew."

"But we were going to investigate it anyway," Jake protested.

"We both know that, but Gabby didn't."

"Remind me never to cross you," Jake said with a smile.

"I'd be happy to, anytime you get close to the line," I said as Jake turned right. "Where are we going now?"

"We need to find Bob Greene and Jim Burr. I want to talk to them."

"Before the chief gets to them?" I asked.

"You're the one who uncovered the fact that Sully didn't trust them, but you have to believe that the chief has already spoken with them, anyway. I'd say that we were entitled to have the first crack at them now that we have new information, wouldn't you?"

"We both know that wasn't our agreement," I said as I handed him my phone.

"What am I supposed to do with this?" he asked as he looked at it.

"Call Stephen Grant and make sure that Gabby's talked to him."

Jake pulled over and parked the truck. "And if she has?"

"Then get his permission for us to track down a lead or two ourselves."

"Is that the way this is going to work?" Jake asked with a slight grimace.

"Welcome to my world," I said as I hit the chief's number

on speed dial.

Jake had a lot to learn about investigating on the side, but I knew that he'd catch on quickly, and I was more than happy to be his teacher.

Chapter 6

"Let me put this on speaker so we can both speak with him," Jake said after he studied my phone for a second.

"My cellphone will actually do that?" I asked him.

"Suzanne, it's amazing what phones will do these days if you know how to use them."

"I just use it to make regular calls," I said. "But I know that Grace can practically launch missiles with hers."

"Hello?" Chief Grant asked from the speaker. "Suzanne, is that you?"

"I'm here, and so is Jake," I said loudly. "Can you hear us okay?"

"It would be easier if you stopped shouting," he said. "What can I do for you?"

"Did Gabby find you yet?" I asked him, modulating my volume a little.

"She just left. Thanks for sending her my way."

"You're welcome," I said.

"Chief," Jake cut in, "we need to know our boundaries on this. Should we leave all of the suspects for you, or is there at least one person we can speak with?"

"Actually, you can go ahead and take a run at Bob Greene and Jim Burr. I spoke with them before Gabby came forward."

"Did you have any luck getting an alibi out of either one of them?" Jake asked him.

"They said that they were together on another job site across town at the time of the murder," the chief said.

"That should be easy enough to check."

"Not if they were the only two subcontractors at the site," Chief Grant answered. "I've got a sneaking suspicion that they were ready for me when I asked them, as though they'd planned it out ahead of time. Only why would they do that if they didn't have something to hide, right?"

"That's my instinct as well," Jake said. "We'd be happy to see if we can rattle them a little on our end."

"Fine, but remember, neither one of you has any official status in the case. You have to tiptoe around your questions."

"That's why I'm here," I said with a grin, "to remind him of that."

"Suzanne, I understand that you spoke with Grace earlier," the chief said, his displeasure clear in his voice.

His statement surprised me. "Am I not allowed to talk to my best friend these days?"

"Of course you can. Just don't push her, okay?"

I understood his reasons for trying to protect his girlfriend, but not from me. "Stephen Grant, I've known you since you were a child, so don't you dare try to tell me how to behave. I don't care if you're the chief of police or the emperor of Mars, when it comes to Grace, I'll do as I please."

Instead of getting upset, Chief Grant just chuckled. "What are you going to do if I disregard your orders and tell you how to act anyway?"

"Gosh, I thought you liked eating donuts at my shop," I said sweetly, making sure that he could hear my smile shine through my voice.

"Is that a threat, Suzanne?"

"No, sir. Think of it more like a promise."

There was a pause, and then he said softly, "I hear you," and then the interim police chief hung up.

Jake was frowning at me as he handed my phone back. "You were a little hard on him, weren't you?"

"Funny, I thought I took it easy on him. Stephen Grant might be her boyfriend, but Grace and I are sisters in every way that matters. I figured it would be easier to smack him with a newspaper and rub his nose in it early so he wouldn't do it again than to have that particular conversation with him again."

"I don't think you're going to have to worry about that happening," Jake said with a smile. "You know, you sounded a bit like your mother just then on the phone as you were scolding him."

I grinned back at him. "I'm not quite sure how you meant that, but I'm going to take it as a compliment, anyway."

"Good, because that was exactly how it was meant to be taken," he said. "Now that we've got a green light, let's say we go tackle Sully's two employees."

"That sounds good to me. I wonder where we can find them," I said.

"I suppose we could check the bars around the area."

"That's a bit of a stereotype, isn't it?" I asked him. "Just because they are blue-collar workers doesn't mean that they drink every day after work."

"Normally I'd agree with you, but their boss was just murdered, so I've got a hunch they might be mourning his loss about now, and I know a lot of men who aren't afraid to drown their troubles in a bottle."

"Point taken," I said. "Besides, what have we got to lose doing it your way? Let's try the closest bar."

Ultimately, I had to admit that I wasn't all that surprised when we found the two men sitting side by side in the nearest bar, both wearing their red-and-black-checked flannel shirts from work. The sight of their attire reminded me of seeing their boss earlier, and I felt a knot grow in my stomach. One thing was certain; Jake had good instincts. He couldn't have been a top-notch investigator for the state police without them.

"Hey, guys," I said as we approached them at a table near the back of the bar. Jim had his feet up on an empty chair beside them–I could see his shiny new pair of cowboy boots–while Bob had on an old leather bomber's jacket. "Do you mind if we join you?"

"Sorry, but this is a private party," Bob said, staring down at his drink without looking up.

"I understand that," I said, "but you're not the only two people in April Springs who are going to miss Sully

Jackson."

Jim looked up from his drink and frowned. "I've never seen you in here before, Suzanne." He appeared to be the drunker of the two by far, and I wondered if he'd started drinking before his partner had arrived on the scene.

"I'm more of a tea drinker myself," I said. "Have you gentlemen met my husband?" I asked as I turned to Jake, who had stayed a step behind me. "Jake Bishop, this is Bob Greene and Jim Burr. They worked for Sully."

"Worked with him was more like it," Bob said as he shook my husband's hand. "He was about to make us partners in the business."

"Is that so?" Jake asked him. "Then I'm doubly sorry for your loss."

"Thanks," Jim replied as he shook his hand in turn.

"Can we buy you both a round in honor of your boss?" Jake asked as he took a seat without being invited. Before they could reply, he waved to the waitress, who came over instantly. "Two more for them, please."

"Aren't you drinking, either?" Jim asked a little testily.

"Not at the moment," Jake said as he pulled out his wallet.

"If you're too good to drink with us, then we'll pay for our own," Jim snapped as he reached into his shirt pocket and started to pull out a roll of bills. I hadn't been meant to see it, but I'd caught a glimpse before Bob knocked his hand away.

"Don't be that way," Bob said. "If the man wants to buy us a drink, then we'll graciously accept his kind offer. That's the problem with you, buddy. You can be a mean drunk sometimes."

"I'm not drunk," Jim protested, his words slurring a little as he spoke.

Bob looked at his friend, and then he shook his head. "Well, even if you aren't, I'm heading that way fast myself." He turned to Jake for a moment and said, "Thanks for the offer, but on second thought, we'll pass." Then, slapping his coworker on the shoulder, Bob said, "Come on, pal. It's time to go."

"We just need a minute of your time," I said as the two men stood a little unsteadily.

"Sorry, but it's going to have to be later," Bob said. Up until then he'd been pretty good at hiding his own level of intoxication, but that façade was slipping quickly away. Clearly both men needed to sober up.

"Neither one of you should be driving," Jake said. "At least let us drive you home." How did he propose to do that? We were in Jake's truck, and there was no way that the four of us were about to fit in the front cab. It was a real working truck, with a single bench seat up front, and not one of the fancier newer models that looked more like cars than trucks on the inside. This was even more exaggerated by its extended bed, a full eight feet long. Jake was proud of the fact that he could lay a sheet of plywood down in back without lowering the tailgate, a reason to brag that was completely lost on me. It seemed to matter to him, though, so that was all that really counted.

"No, thanks. Stella will give us a ride," Jim said as he threw a fifty-dollar bill down on the table. It appeared that the men had been celebrating for a while. "What do you say?" he asked her as she approached us. It was clear that she'd been keeping her eye on us ever since we'd walked through the door.

"Sure thing, boys. I'd be happy to do it. My shift just ended," the waitress said as she scooped up the money. Was she sweet on one of the two men? I had to believe that it was plausible, given the way that she'd kept looking at them.

"Guys, if we don't talk now, it's just going to happen later," Jake said in his most officious voice. "It's your call, but it's going to happen, one way or the other."

"Then later it will be," Jim said, and the two men left the bar together, following the waitress outside into the dusky evening.

"Let's go," Jake told me quickly the moment the three of them started walking toward the parking lot.

"Are we going to follow them?" I asked.

"We really don't have much choice, do we? I don't think we'll get much out of them this evening, but who knows, maybe we'll get lucky," Jake said as we headed for his truck. "How do you do it, Suzanne?"

"How do I do what?" I asked as we got in and took off in their general direction. "Jake, are you sure that it's a good idea to follow them?"

"If nothing else, it might help us to know where they are going next," he said.

"Hang on a second and go back. How do I do what?"

"Get folks to talk to you like that," he said as he caught up with them, and then trailed back a little. His truck wasn't exactly inconspicuous, so he had to keep his distance in order not to be spotted. "I've always depended on being able to compel suspects to talk to me, but you've never had that tool at your disposal."

"Mostly I try my best to be sympathetic to their problems," I said. "It's important to remember that just about everyone I speak to about a murder is innocent, and usually they are in mourning, too."

"I can see that, but I doubt that I'll ever be able to master that particular technique," he said.

"Do you mind if I ask you something? Do you miss having a badge and a gun?" I asked him.

"Well, we both know that I'm still armed and carrying a weapon," he said as he patted his jacket.

"You know what I meant," I said.

He thought about that for a few seconds before he answered. "If I'm being honest, sometimes I do, but then I remember all of the nightmares of my old job, and I get over it pretty quickly."

"You could always do something else in the law enforcement line, you know."

Jake glanced over at me and grinned. "Are you getting tired of having me underfoot so soon, Suzanne?"

"Of course not," I said as I reached over and squeezed his

arm. "I just don't want you to be bored."

"With you around, I don't see how that's ever going to happen," he said with an easy smile.

I was about to comment again when I saw brake lights going on ahead of us. "It appears that one of our suspects is being dropped off."

"The question is which one, though."

We pulled into an open space on the street a hundred feet away and saw Bob Greene get out, stop and wave to the occupants of the car, and then make his way into a small duplex. Stella and Jim drove off, and after noting where we were, Jake followed them discreetly.

"The next question is, are they going to Jim's or Stella's?" Jake asked.

"Do you think they're actually a couple?" I asked.

"No, but from the way Stella was looking at him back at the bar, I think she'd like them to be," Jake said. "When I glanced over at her, I saw her looking at him like a wolf checking out a steak."

"Wow, that's a vivid way of putting it."

"What can I say? I have a way with words," Jake replied with a slight smile, keeping his focus intently on the road ahead of us.

After a few minutes, I saw brake lights again. "It appears that we're here, wherever that might be," I said.

"I'm guessing one of them lives there," Jake said as he pointed to a modest house in a quiet neighborhood.

He was wrong, though, something we found out soon enough.

Chapter 7

"Come out and face me, you murderer!" Jim Burr screamed as he tumbled out of Stella's car and faced the house. He was making no effort at all to mask the fact that he was drunk. "You killed him, didn't you?"

"Jim, be quiet! You don't even live here, do you?" Stella asked as she grabbed his arm. "Get back in the car. You're not in any shape to do this! I need to take you home right now."

"I'm not going anywhere until I've said what I have to say," he said as he pulled his arm free from her grasp. Jim faced the house again and shouted, "I'm not leaving. Do you hear me?"

In the growing darkness, I saw the front door open and a slim woman in her mid-fifties come out. Wearing a familiar patterned robe of red and black checks, she was holding a heavy wrench in her hand, one big enough to defend herself or attack any aggressors. "What do you want, Jim?"

"Why'd you kill him, Shirley?" he asked, his voice softening as he spoke. "He was a good guy, and he deserved better than what he got."

"You're drunk," she said, stating the obvious to anyone within earshot of his earlier shouts. "Go home."

"Not until I get an answer," Jim insisted. "Was it because he didn't love you? Is that any reason to do what you did?"

"You don't know what you're talking about," Shirley answered, but it was clear that his accusation had hit home by the sudden redness in her cheeks. "I'm not going to tell you again. Get off my property, or you're going to be sorry."

"What are you going to do, kill me, too?" Jim challenged her, his voice becoming aggressive again.

Shirley must have realized that it was useless talking to Jim in his condition. Instead, she turned to Stella and ordered, "If you don't do something about this right now, I'm going to have to handle it, and believe me, he's not going to be happy if I have to defend myself."

"I'm trying," Stella whined as she continued to plead with the man. He continued to ignore her, and then he started unsteadily toward Shirley.

"This has gone far enough," Jake said tersely as he got out of the truck.

"You're not a cop anymore, remember?" I reminded him as I got out, too.

"That doesn't matter right now," he said as he took a few purposeful strides toward the conflict. "Get in the car, Jim," he ordered the drunk when he got close enough to him.

The man looked startled by his presence. "What are you doing here?"

"I'm trying to keep you from getting yourself killed," Jake said firmly. He took Jim's arm, and though the electrician tried to pull away, Jake's grip was quite a bit stronger than Stella's had been. As much as the drunken man struggled, Jake didn't even appear to notice. Jake pulled the man toward Stella's car clearly against his will, and when Jim resisted, Jake leaned forward and whispered something into his ear.

It sobered him in an instant, and he immediately stopped struggling.

After Jake had him in the car, Stella said, "Thank you so much."

"Just get him home," Jake said.

She nodded as she got into the driver's seat. "I promise."

After they were gone, I approached Jake. "What did you say to him?"

"I'll tell you later," he said as Shirley neared us.

"Who exactly are you, anyway?" she asked him.

"I'm Jake Bishop, and this is my wife, Suzanne," he said.

"I've known Suzanne for years. It's you I don't recognize." A look of comprehension suddenly appeared on her face. "You must be the ex-state cop I heard about. Well,

I'm not sure why you interceded, but thanks for doing it."

She turned back to face the house and was heading for the door when Jake said, "Shirley, we weren't here by accident."

The electrician whipped around and stared at him. "Let me get this straight. You're not a cop anymore, are you?"

"I'm retired," Jake admitted.

"If you're retired, then why were you following him around town?" she asked as she gestured toward where Stella's car had been.

"Let's just say that I've taken a personal interest in Sully Jackson's murder," Jake said. "Jim seemed to think that you might have had something to do with what happened to him."

I could see her grip clench a little on the wrench. "And you actually believed him? It would have been clear to a blind man tonight that he was drunk."

"Maybe so, but we've heard that he might not have been all that far off the mark with what he said. Were you and Sully really in talks to merge?"

"Sure, our business, not our love lives," she said, the frustration clear in her voice. "Why does everyone keep saying that he turned me down?"

"Are you saying that you weren't interested in him romantically?" I asked.

Shirley started to deny it, but after a moment, it was clear that she'd decided to come clean with us. "The truth is that I asked him out on a date again. We went out a few months ago, but it kind of all just fizzled out. I decided to try to light the fire again, you know? He said no, and that's the end of the story. Haven't you ever been rejected? It's not the end of the world when it happens."

"No, but sometimes it can feel as though it might be," I said sympathetically.

"Maybe so, but not this time. I liked Sully, even after he turned me down. The truth is that I never would have killed him, and if I ever find out who did, they'd better hope that I'm not the first person to get to them."

"So then you wouldn't mind helping us find the murderer,

would you?" I asked her.

The question caught her a little off-guard. "What can I do? I'm just an electrician."

"You could start by telling us where you were at the time of the murder," Jake replied.

"I don't even know when he was killed."

"Five minutes after three this afternoon," I supplied.

"That's pretty exact," Shirley said. "How could you possibly know when it happened that precisely?"

"We were fifty feet away when it happened," Jake answered.

She was shocked by the news. "If you were so close, why didn't you stop it from happening?"

"I tried," Jake replied heavily, "but there was nothing I could do. The killer got away before I could catch them."

"You must not have been a very good cop, were you?" she asked.

"He was the best of the best," I responded in anger. Nobody was going to criticize my husband in front of me and get away with it.

"Have you been in the old wagon factory lately? It's not exactly open space over there," Jake said.

"Tell me about it," she said.

"So, you're admitting that you've been there before," I said.

"Of course I have. I bid on the job, too, but your mother gave it to Sully instead."

"How did that make you feel?" I asked her, looking for some sign that I was getting to her.

She just shrugged. "The truth is that I get more jobs than I lose. After all, it's just business."

"Tell me about your alibi," Jake gently reminded her. "Where were you when he died?"

"Let's see. At around three? I must have been in my office working a bid up for a job in Union Square; that's what I was doing for most of the afternoon today."

"Can anyone vouch for you?" I asked.

"No, I was by myself."

"Are you saying that you didn't make any calls or have any visitors at all?" Jake asked her.

"Sorry I don't have anyone to confirm it, but I thought only guilty people had alibis."

"You'd be surprised," Jake said cryptically. "When exactly was the last time that you saw Sully alive?"

She thought about it for a moment, frowned, and then she said, "You're going to find out sooner or later, so I might as well tell you myself. We had breakfast together this morning."

"Where was this?" I asked.

"At the Boxcar," she said. "Only I should tell you that it didn't go all that well."

"What happened?" Jake asked her.

"We had a hitch in our negotiations," Shirley admitted. "Sully said a few things, and I did, too. I'm afraid that it might have looked bad to anyone who didn't know us."

So, she was admitting that she'd seen the murder victim earlier that day, and that they'd quarreled in a public place. It wasn't a bad strategy for her to volunteer the information to us before we found out on our own. Was she offering an explanation or trying to dissipate a potential storm before it hit?

"Listen, I've got to go back inside," Shirley said. "I've helped you all that I can."

"Thanks for your cooperation," Jake said. "We'll probably be in touch later."

She looked aggravated by that, but she didn't comment.

After Shirley was back inside and we were headed toward Jake's truck, I said, "That was pretty slick."

"What, the way I handled things?" he asked with a grin.

"That, too, but I was talking more about the way Shirley got that damaging information about her meeting with Sully this morning out in the open so quickly."

"As a strategy, it's not all that bad," Jake agreed. "We should tell Grant what we just learned," he added as he reached for his phone before getting back into the truck.

I put a hand on his before he could dial, though.

"What is it, Suzanne?"

"Before you make that call, I want to know what you said to Jim Burr to get him to settle down so quickly."

Jake smiled. "I told him that if he kept fighting me, I might have to break his arm."

"You threatened him?" I asked, incredulous that my husband could do something like that, and so calmly to boot.

"Suzanne, the man was getting ready to take a swing at me. I could feel him tense up, so I decided I should probably warn him that attacking me was a very bad idea."

"Would you have done it, though?" I asked him.

"Of course not," Jake answered. "The threat was enough, just like I was sure that it would be."

"But if he had attacked you even after you warned him, what then?"

"I wouldn't have had much choice, would I?" Jake asked. "I would have been forced to defend myself."

I thought about that for a moment, and then I said, "There's steel in you that surprises me sometimes."

Jake sighed before he spoke again. "I don't know what to tell you. I had a tough job, and it made me learn what I was willing to do and what I wasn't."

"And there's no way to turn that off now that you're retired, is there?" I asked him.

"Sorry, it's a part of me that I wouldn't change, even if I could."

"I get that," I said. "I'm just glad you're on my side."

"So am I," he said with a grin. "Now, can I make that call?"

"I'm not going to try to stop you," I said with a smile of my own. As Jake brought the chief up to speed on what we had learned, I marveled at just how complex my husband really was. Though we'd been married for quite a while, I realized that there were parts of him that I didn't know all that well yet, but I vowed to change that. Nothing he'd told me had made me love him any less. He was a man of honor and integrity, and that was a part of what made him so special to me, but there was a strength underlying it all that I had to acknowledge as well.

Chapter 8

After Jake brought the police chief up to date on the latest developments in our investigation, he hung up and turned to me. "You know something? This might just work out."

"The marriage?" I asked him with a smile.

"That's beyond question," he answered with a smile of his own. "I'm talking about our new arrangement. There's something to be said for working the case from this side."

"Believe me, it's not always this easy," I told him. "There are lots of times I hit brick walls when no one will say anything to me about the case I'm working on, and I can't exactly compel them to talk."

"I understand that," Jake said, "but it's nice when it happens, isn't it?"

Once we were back in the truck, I replied, "It's wonderful, but tonight we were in the right place at the right time to witness what happened between Jim and Shirley, and that led to everything else that we learned here."

"Suzanne, don't underestimate us. After all, we were here because we were following a lead. You should be happier than you seem to be about what we uncovered tonight."

"I'm pleased, but we have a long way to go before we're ready to name the killer."

"And no one knows that better than I do," Jake said as he leaned over and patted my leg gently. As he drove, I noticed that he wasn't heading back to our cottage.

"Are we still working on the case?" I asked as I glanced at my watch. "Because if we are, I should remind you that I can't stay out much later. I have a donut shop to run in the morning, remember?"

"I'm not about to forget that," Jake replied. "There's something that's been bothering me about the crime scene though, and if you don't mind, I'd like to swing by there and check it out before we quit for the night. What do you say?"

"What makes you think that Griffin is gone?"

"I don't know one way or the other, but there's only one way to find out. Is it okay?"

I knew how I was when I was on a case, chewing on it like a dog with a bone, and it didn't surprise me that Jake was the same way. After all, he'd been in the crime-solving business a lot longer than I'd been. "That's fine."

"Thanks. I won't keep you out too late. I promise."

When we got there, I wasn't all that surprised to see that Griffin was still stationed out front. "That's too bad," I said. "Hey, why are you parking the truck?"

"I want a word with him. Don't worry; it won't take a second," Jake said as he started to get out of the truck.

"Hang on a second. I'm coming with you," I said.

He just shrugged, which was enough agreement for me.

"Getting chilly out, isn't it?" Jake asked as he approached the policeman.

"I could use a cup of coffee," Griffin said. "You don't happen to have any on you, do you?"

"Sorry, we don't, but we could go get you some," Jake volunteered. "Suzanne, would you mind?" he asked as he tried to hand me his truck keys.

"You're kidding, right? I'm not driving your truck," I said, refusing his offer, "but I don't mind if you go."

"Never mind," Griffin said. "I'm due to be relieved in twenty minutes anyway."

"Are you guarding the building around the clock?" Jake asked him.

"We're here until the chief says otherwise," the officer answered.

"Well, have a good night then," Jake said as he saluted with two fingers.

Griffin grinned. "In about twenty-one minutes, I will."

As we got back into the truck and headed back home, I asked, "Were you trying to get rid of me back there?"

"No, ma'am," he said, smiling.

"I should hope not," I said. "We're a team, remember?"

"Hey, you spoke with Gabby without me. How come that's okay, but me talking to another cop by myself isn't?"

I thought about it for a second, and then I realized that he had a legitimate point. "You're right. I'm wrong."

"I'm sorry; I missed that. Would you mind repeating it?"

"As a matter of fact, I would," I said. "Next time I'll go."

"Even if it means driving my truck?" Jake asked playfully.

"Only if you're okay if something happens to it while I'm driving."

"On second thought, I'll run the errands myself."

I looked at the ancient truck. "What is it about this truck that makes you love it so much?"

"I thought I told you. It was my dad's," Jake said softly. "When he died, it was about the sum total of my inheritance from him, but it was all that I ever really wanted. Whenever I drive it, I think of him."

I had had no idea. "I get it, Jake. I'm sorry about all of the disparaging comments I've made about it in the past."

"You haven't said that many bad things about her," Jake said as he stroked the dashboard.

"Maybe not to your face," I replied. "The sniping stops now, though."

"Thanks. This truck is a part of me, good, bad, or indifferent."

"And I'm sure that I'll grow to love it, too."

"Well, I wouldn't expect you to go that far," he answered with a hint of laughter. I knew how hard it was for Jake to open up to me, and I considered it a real victory that he'd told me the story behind his truck.

"She and I will at least learn to share you," I said as I stroked the seat between us.

"That's all that I ask," Jake said. "Let's get you home. I'm getting hungry, how about you?"

"In all the excitement, we forgot to eat, didn't we? Would you mind if we just have sandwiches at the cottage? I hate to eat a big meal just before I go to bed."

"That sounds perfect to me," Jake said. "We have one more stop to make, and then we'll head home."

"Why do we have to stop? We have all the fixings we need to make sandwiches," I protested. It really was getting late, at least for me.

"I know that, but we need something from your mother."

"What's that?" I asked.

"A key to the factory," Jake replied. "Once the police chief clears it, I need to get back in there."

I knew there was no sense trying to argue with him. Besides, I wanted that key myself. "Fine, but we're not staying long."

"I promise," he said, but I knew that I wouldn't be able to hold him to that. He didn't have the urgency to get home that I did, and why should he? My husband could sleep in as late as he wanted to, not that he would, especially while he was working on a murder investigation, but at least he had the option. Before long, I'd have to be getting up and going in to work while the world slept around me. It was getting harder and harder to drag myself into work some days while Jake stayed behind, warm and comfy in our bed. Still, I was a donutmaker by profession as well as by choice, and the hours came with the job.

"What are you two doing out so late?" Momma asked as she answered the door to her home. "Suzanne, shouldn't you be asleep by now?"

"We're headed home to get a bite, and then I'm going straight to bed," I admitted. "We need a favor first, though."

"Are you out of food? You really should keep your pantry stocked. Lucky for you I made a pot roast tonight, and we have plenty for all four of us."

"Thanks, but we can't stay," I said, and then I looked over and saw the smile on my husband's face as he took a deep whiff of the aromas coming from my mother's kitchen.

"Are you sure?" Jake asked. "Dot, that smells awfully good."

"Suzanne, how can you deprive your husband of a hot meal?" Momma asked me.

"You might as well throw in the towel, Suzanne," Phillip said from the hallway. "You're clearly outnumbered."

I could see the wisdom in his advice. "When you're right, you're right. Thanks, we appreciate it, Momma."

"Don't be silly. It's our pleasure." She turned to her husband. "Phillip, do me a favor and set two more places at the table."

"With pleasure," he said, and then the former police chief winked at me and grinned. We'd had our share of battles in the past, but I'd come around to begin to see some of what my mother saw in him, and despite our earlier conflicts, I was genuinely beginning to like the man.

"Do you need a hand?" Jake asked him.

"You bet. While we're working, you can bring me up to speed on your investigation."

"Gentlemen, must we speak of murder all of the time?" Momma asked them.

"It's better to let them get it out of their systems before we eat," I told her, and Jake grinned at me as the two men disappeared into the dining room.

"It's sweet of you to feed us, but I really do have plenty of food at home," I told Momma after the men were gone.

"I know that," she answered with a smile. "How have you been? The truth is that I miss seeing you every day. When we lived together at the cottage, I could always count on it."

"I know. I miss you, too, but to be fair, you got married first and moved away."

She smiled. "And it turned out to be the second-best decision I ever made in my life."

"Do I dare ask what the first one was? Having me, perhaps?" I asked her with a grin.

"You were a direct result of it, so in a way, yes, but I meant marrying your father."

"Shouldn't you keep your voice down when you say that?" I asked her. "After all, Phillip is just in the other room."

"He knows how I feel about him, and it's a discussion we had long ago. Suzanne, there's room in my heart to love more than one person, just as there is in Jake's."

"But just one at a time, right?" I asked her, smiling.

She laughed. "In that way, yes, but never forget that I love you, too," Momma said as she startled me by hugging me.

"I love you, too," I answered.

After we broke away, she asked, "So, if you didn't come by for a meal, what brings you here, not that you need an excuse to visit?"

"We'd like a key to the factory," I said. "It's either that or we break in, and I thought you'd prefer it this way."

Momma frowned. "Chief Grant told me specifically that the building was off limits until further notice. You aren't planning on sneaking there in spite of his orders, are you?"

"Would I do that?" I asked her as I laughed a bit.

"Suzanne."

"Relax, Momma. Jake wants to look around as soon as the chief releases the crime scene."

"Have you made any progress in your investigation?"

"We haven't had that much opportunity yet. Sully was just murdered this afternoon," I said.

"I know. These things take time."

"They do." I wasn't about to bring my mother up to date on what Jake and I had done so far, but then again, I had to tell her something, because I was pretty sure that my husband was bringing the former chief up to speed in the next room. "We've found several suspects, and interviewed three of them already. There's a fourth that we're going to speak with tomorrow."

Momma looked surprised by our progress. "But that's wonderful. Who's in the running?"

I could tell from the glint in her eye that she was eager to know the details, so it was time to sing for our supper. "So far, we have Bob Greene and Jim Burr. They were Sully's two employees. Then there's Shirley Edam. She wanted to merge their operations, both business and personal, though she's denying it at the moment. We've already had preliminary interviews with the three of them."

"Who's left on your list?"

"Carl Descent," I said.

"Carl? You're kidding. Why on earth would he want to kill Sully?"

"The prevailing theory is that he wanted to punish both of you for stealing the building out from under him," I told her. "We heard that Sully was a deciding factor in who the owner sold the place to."

Momma's face went ashen. "Is this a credible motive?"

"I don't know. You tell me."

She paused a moment as she considered it. "Carl has a temper, and he can be vindictive, too. I knew that he'd be upset when I got the building and he didn't, but why would he kill Sully? His recommendation to the seller just doesn't seem as though it's enough reason to commit murder."

"I know, but that's what we're going to find out," I said.

"May I ask you how were you able to come up with four names so quickly?" she asked me.

"We have a source," I said, hedging my bets.

Momma shook her head before she spoke. "There's only one person in April Springs I know of who could have come up with four such disparate names in such short order. You spoke with Gabby Williams, didn't you?"

I smiled at her. "Sorry, but I cannot either confirm or deny that," I said.

"You don't have to," Momma said. After a moment, she added softly, "Gabby's not exactly neutral when it comes to Sully. They were seeing each other, you know."

"I just found out about it, but how did you know?" It never ceased to amaze me how much my mother knew about the folks we lived amongst.

"I have sources of my own," she said as she walked over to her purse and retrieved a key. It had a paper tag on it that said WAGON WHEEL, and she handed it to me. "Just return it when you're finished with it, please."

"Thanks, I will," I said as I slipped it into my front jeans pocket.

"Is it time to eat yet, Dot?" Phillip asked as the two men came out of the dining room together.

"We were just waiting for you two to finish setting the table," Momma said.

No more was said about the murder the rest of the evening, and despite the hour, I had a lovely time. Dinner was magnificent, which was no real surprise, and the company was delightful. Phillip entertained us with a story from one of the old newspapers he'd stumbled across about a family of chipmunks that had nestled in an old man's beard when it got cold, and his retelling of the tale had us all laughing by the time he finished. I hated to break things up, but after the third time I tried to hide a yawn, Momma said, "Suzanne, you have an early day tomorrow. Don't mind these dishes. Phillip and I will take care of them."

"Are you sure?" I protested, but it had to be clear to everyone there that it wasn't all that sincere.

"Positive," she said.

Jake looked inquiringly at me, and I nodded slightly. He shook Phillip's hand, and then hugged my mother. "Dot, it was all wonderful. Thank you."

"You're very welcome," she said.

Before we got to the truck, Jake said, "We forgot to get the key."

I patted my pocket. "I took care of it. We got a great deal more than that, didn't we? I'm stuffed. I can't believe how much I ate."

"Will you still be able to get to sleep when we get home?" he asked.

"Are you kidding? You might have to carry me inside after I pass out on the ride home."

"I can do that," he said. "They're good together, aren't they?"

"I have to admit that they're growing on me," I answered sleepily.

I managed to stumble into the cottage on my own power, but just barely, and I was asleep before my head hit the pillow. It had been a big day, and tomorrow would be even crazier, but for the moment, all I cared about was sleeping during the little time I had left before I had to get up and go to work.

Chapter 9

Jake was still asleep when I left the cottage the next morning, which was a very good thing as far as I was concerned. He'd tried once to keep my hours, but we'd both known that it had been a mistake, and he'd never done it again. As I drove the short distance to the donut shop in the dark, I kept thinking about the wagon factory. Was there still a guard posted there, or had the police chief opened it back up? I had the key with me, so I could look around myself if I wanted to before work. Jake had forgotten to ask me for it, and I knew that he'd be retrieving it the moment he realized that I still had it in my possession. Why not get a little sleuthing in before I started my day at the donut shop, if that was the case?

I decided to keep going past Donut Hearts and drove to the wagon factory.

No one was posted out front, and there was no sign of a squad car there, either.

I parked my Jeep and got out, but halfway up the steps, I glanced up toward the second floor windows and saw something that stopped me in my tracks.

A small light was bobbing up and down up there, flickering as it passed the windows closest to the street.

I knew that the place wasn't haunted, no matter how many stories folks around April Springs told about the ghostly caretaker that supposedly roamed the building after midnight.

Someone was up there, and I was determined to find out who it was.

I wasn't going in unarmed, though. I didn't have my trusty softball bat with me, but I had the next best thing, a jack handle that would serve to defend me just fine. My Jeep had gone through some serious trauma at the hands of a snowy road before, and I could have used a little protection back then, but I'd failed to collect it before I'd fled into the woods. That wasn't going to happen again.

Grabbing the handle, I started toward the door, ready for whatever I might find upstairs. There was still police tape across the front façade, but someone had carefully slit it open in order to pass through. I tried the door, and to my surprise, I found it unlocked! I knew the police would have secured it before leaving, so whoever was up there had used a key, making the one in my pocket unnecessary. How had they gotten it? Did any of the workers have access to the building during off-hours, thus needing a key, or was this someone else entirely? Pushing the door open, I prepared myself for anything.

I had walked just three steps inside when I heard someone directly above me, moving or dragging something across the floor over my head.

What was I doing? Had I completely lost my mind? I always shouted at the heroines in horror movies who did the exact same thing that I was doing right now. I wasn't sure where the false bravado had come from, but I'd never forgive myself if I wound up dead because of my own stupidity.

This was something I shouldn't be doing without any backup.

I had to get out of there until I could get someone on the scene to make sure that I survived this.

I never even considered calling the police. It was a simple matter of calling Jake and waiting for him to answer. When he finally picked up, it was clear that I'd woken him from a deep sleep. "Jake, I'm at the wagon factory."

"What are you doing there?" he asked me groggily.

"I thought I'd drive by before work. The thing is that someone beat me to it."

That got his attention. "Are they still there?"

"As far as I can tell. As I drove up, I saw a light coming from the second story, and when I snuck in, I heard someone moving boxes or something upstairs."

"You're still in the building? Get out!"

"Relax. I'm standing out on the front stoop," I said. "But you'd better hurry. I don't want whoever is up there to get away."

"Don't move. I'll be there in three minutes."

I started to tell him that he could barely drive that far in that amount of time, even if he were fully dressed, but my phone was dead at that point. He'd hung up on me.

Now what should I do? I was tempted to slink back to my Jeep and wait there, ready to escape if whoever was inside decided to come out. Then again, I needed to be sure that I could identify them. I finally decided to compromise by moving over to the bushes by the front entrance. I was out of the line of sight of the door, but I could still run if I was spotted.

Two minutes later, Jake drove toward the building, shutting off his headlights as he coasted the last twenty feet. That was smart of him, something that I'd failed to do. He came up to me quickly in the darkness, and I had to wonder how he'd known that I was there.

"How did you spot me?" I asked in a whisper, though there was no way that anyone would be able to hear me. "I thought I was hidden pretty well."

"The tire iron in your hand caught my headlights before I shut them off," he said. "Has there been any movement up there since you called me?"

At least he wasn't scolding me. I considered that a victory in my book. "Not that I've been able to see. Listen, I didn't mean to push my luck walking into the building by myself. As soon as I came to my senses, I got out and called you."

"That's all that matters," my husband said as he pulled out his handgun. "I don't suppose there's a chance in the world you'd be willing to stay out here while I go in alone, is there?"

"What do you think?"

"Just stay behind me, then," he ordered, a command that I had no problems complying with.

Together, we walked into the building single file, and then we headed slowly up the stairs.

We were halfway there when we both heard the back door slam on the first floor behind us. Blast it all, whoever had been there had moved downstairs from the second floor while I'd been outside waiting on Jake, and now they'd gotten away. We were still racing for the back door when we heard someone screech their tires as they drove quickly away. "I can't believe that we missed them again," I said in disgust. "I should have followed my first instincts and gone after whoever it was by myself."

"No, you shouldn't have," Jake said. "You were right to call me."

"But now whoever was here is gone."

"Maybe so, but if we got lucky, we might still find something. They must have heard you earlier, so they could have left before they were able to find what they were looking for." We walked back up the stairs together, and Jake stopped me at the top as he knelt down and studied the floor with his flashlight.

"What do you see?" I asked him, straining to catch a glimpse of whatever he was looking at.

"Footprints," he said as he pointed to a dusty edge.

"Does that mean that we can't investigate?" I asked him.

"No. Just be careful where you put your feet, and try to match my footsteps as closely as you can." He moved to the edge of the floor along the outside wall and started toward the main area. "Suzanne, where exactly did you hear that noise before?"

"It had to be somewhere over there," I said, pointing to a small room that must have been an office once upon a time when the factory had still been a going concern. "It's right above where I was standing."

"Come on. Let's check it out," Jake said, carefully walking toward it. As he drew the door open, I held my breath. What would we find there? Was it another body? I hoped with all of my heart that it wasn't, but given my history, I knew that I couldn't bank on it.

I let out a deep sigh of relief when I realized that the room was empty, at least of people, dead or otherwise.

Instead, there were half a dozen wooden crates of varying sizes stacked in there, clearly recently disturbed. "Do you think there's something inside of one of these?" I asked Jake, still whispering for some odd reason.

He was about to answer when another flashlight beam illuminated the area where we stood.

"Drop your weapon," a voice commanded from the darkness, and I had to wonder if whoever had been there before had circled back to get the drop on us.

Chapter 10

Jake didn't immediately comply with the command, and I wondered if he was going to take a stand and have a shootout right then and there. Instead, he held his hands up in the air as he said, "Everything's okay. It's just us, Chief."

"Jake, what are you two doing here?" the acting police chief asked as he reached over and turned on an overhead light.

"Suzanne saw someone wandering around up here as she was driving past, so she called me," he explained.

"Is there any reason that you didn't think of calling me first?" he asked me as he frowned. "And this place is nowhere near your donut shop."

"Are you honestly all that surprised that I called my husband first?" I asked him. "If it's any consolation, you were next on my list. As to why I was here, I was curious to see if you still had a guard posted outside. I wasn't ignoring you, I promise."

"I wish I could say that it helped, but it doesn't." As he looked around, he asked, "Did you happen to see who it was?"

"Sorry. Whoever it was beat it out of here after they realized that Suzanne must have called for reinforcements."

"So, there's nothing new that you can add to the investigation?" the chief asked, the weariness heavy in his voice.

"I wouldn't say that. There are some pretty good prints in the dust over there," Jake said as he pointed to the stairwell. "But I can't say for sure when they were made."

"We'll get some shots of them anyway," Chief Grant said as he reached for his radio and called in his team. After he'd summoned his staff, I asked, "How did you even know that we were here? Is there some kind of alarm system in the building we don't know about?"

"You'd have to ask your mother that," Chief Grant said. "Someone reported seeing lights coming from the upstairs of the building, so I thought I'd check it out."

"You're working awfully late, aren't you?" I asked him.

"I couldn't sleep," he admitted. "Murder has a way of doing that to me. Suzanne, tell me everything that happened since you first showed up, and don't leave anything out."

I brought him up to date, including being sure to mention that I hadn't been the one who'd cut the crime scene tape. When I was finished, he asked, "I wonder what they were after?"

"I have no idea, but I'd love to get a look inside those crates," I admitted.

"Is that what the tire iron is for?" he asked me.

"This? No, it was more for self-defense, but I don't see why we can't use it to open these, too."

The interim chief laughed. "We'll do this by the book, if you don't mind. Shouldn't you be at the donut shop getting ready for your day?"

I glanced at my watch. "I can push it a few more minutes if I need to."

"Why don't you go on? I'll take over from here," the chief said.

"Don't worry, Suzanne. I'll stop by when we're through here," Jake told me.

The chief looked at him oddly. "Jake, I'm sorry, but you'll have to leave, too. You don't have any official standing here, remember? I hate to be by the book about this, but this is still a crime scene, so no civilians are allowed." He looked at Jake as though he were seeking his approval, and my husband quickly nodded.

"Of course. You're right, Chief. Suzanne, let's get out of here and let the man do his job."

"Thanks for understanding," Chief Grant said.

"You bet," Jake replied.

My husband guided me away from the footprints he'd found earlier, and we were back outside soon enough.

"Ouch. That was kind of harsh," I said.

"You can't blame him. He's just doing his job. If our roles were reversed, I would have done the exact same thing. Do you need a hand at the donut shop this morning?"

"Thanks for offering, but I've got it covered," I told him, surprised by his offer.

"Then if it's all the same to you, I'm going back to bed," my husband said, and then he kissed me. "Thanks for calling me."

"I'm sorry it turned out this way," I said.

"No worries, Suzanne," he replied. I watched him walk back to his truck in the dim light coming from a nearby streetlight. Was he hanging his head down, or was it my imagination? It couldn't have been easy being thrown out of an investigation like that. I made up my mind to make it up to him. Jake had been put in an awkward position because of me, and I didn't like it the least little bit.

He followed me back to the donut shop, and I waved as he drove past me on his way back to our cottage.

For the moment, I needed to forget about murder and who had paid an early-morning visit to the wagon factory.

It was time, yet again, to make more donuts.

Chapter 11

For most people, it might have been difficult to go back to work after what had just happened, but I didn't have any trouble starting my day making donuts as though Jake and I hadn't just been so close to a possible killer. Measuring out flour, sugar, and other ingredients was almost done by muscle-memory at this point. It was time to come up with a new cake donut, so I leafed through my recipe book for different ideas. I'd been meaning to play with savory donuts for some time, but I always seemed to go back to sweet offerings. What would my customers think about a bacon-filled donut with crumbled bacon in the batter and maybe a maple glaze on top? I was fairly certain that my husband would love the outcome, but would anyone else? How about one with ham? And maybe some pineapple frosting spread on it? Someday I'd try something that different, but not today. I kept skimming my recipe book's sections on new ideas, but nothing really caught my eye. Then I remembered that Jake had added a new staple to our pantry at home, one that I'd never tried until he'd come into my life. I knew that he loved the unusual cherry tart spread on toast, so why not try it in a donut? I'd brought some with me a few days before, so I incorporated it into one of my plain donut batters and made half a dozen at the end of the batch. Emma, my assistant, came in as I was glazing one, so I offered her a bite as I grabbed a pinch for myself.

"What do you think?" I asked her as I tasted it for myself. It was dreadful. There was something about the deep-frying process that had somehow curdled the spread.

"It's... interesting," she said after she took a nibble.

I spit out the bit in my mouth, and then I took a deep drink of water. "It's putrid," I said. "Don't you dare start lying to me, young lady."

"Okay, you're right. What was that? I can't believe that I

actually swallowed my bite."

I showed her the container I'd brought from home. "Jake loves this stuff."

"Have you thought about simmering some on the stovetop and using it as a glaze?" Emma asked after she'd bravely tasted a bit of it on the tip of her finger. "It's clearly not suited for being mixed in batter, but it might make a good topping."

"We might try it another day, but for now, I'm sticking to the basics."

"It's always worked for us in the past," Emma said with a grin. "How has your morning been otherwise?"

"More exciting than I normally like," I admitted without thinking as I threw away the rest of the failed experiments.

"Really? What happened?" My assistant was suddenly eager to hear my story, but I knew better than to share it with her. The one bone of contention we ever seemed to have was where her father, the newspaperman, was concerned. A few times in the past, what I'd told Emma in confidence had come back to bite me, and I'd become reluctant to share anything concerning my investigations with her.

"Nothing," I said lamely. "Never mind."

"Is it about the murder? Suzanne, you can trust me. I won't say anything to dad unless you give me your specific approval to share it."

I knew that it wasn't fair to keep holding her past sins against her. "Jake and I were at the wagon factory before work this morning. I swung by on my way over here, and I saw flickering lights coming from the second floor."

"Do you think that it was a ghost?" she asked me with bated breath.

"Most likely it was more like a prowler," I said. "Emma, you don't honestly believe in ghosts, do you?"

"How can you not?" she asked me. "As far as I'm concerned, there are more things going on in this world than can be easily explained or dismissed."

She'd sounded remarkably like Gabby when she'd said it,

and I had to wonder if I'd just run into another true believer in ghosts. "Well, whether you are right or you are wrong, this was no spirit. Someone was there, all right."

"What could they possibly want in an old building being renovated?"

"That's what we were trying to find out," I said.

"Did you have any luck?"

I was willing to share some of the generalities of what had happened, but I wasn't about to mention the crates that had been moved. "Not so much. Whoever was there left before Jake could get there."

"At least you didn't go into the building by yourself," she said. "That could have been really dangerous."

I didn't tell her that I'd done just that before I'd had a sudden change of heart. I decided that it was time to change the subject, so I glanced at the clock. "You're running a little behind schedule this morning, aren't you?"

"Sorry. I don't know how it happened, but my alarm didn't go off. It's amazing to me that I woke up at all."

"More out of habit than anything else, probably."

"I'll stay late today if you'd like me to," she offered.

"I wasn't scolding you, Emma," I said with a smile. "I was just curious."

She looked around at the mess in the kitchen. "Since you're finished dropping the cake donuts, I'll get started on the dishes." As she began to run the warm water in the sink, she asked, "Does this mean I don't get my break?"

"Why would I do that? It would be more like I was being punished if I deprived myself of your company," I said happily. "Half the fun of taking a break is hanging out with you outside, braving the cold temperature together."

"I can't wait until it starts to warm up again," she answered.

"Just wait. In July we'll be wishing for chillier weather again. Just you wait."

"I don't doubt it, but we could use a bit of that heat now, if you ask me." As Emma started washing the pots and pans

I'd used making the earlier batters, I got started on the yeast donuts. No real surprise, I finished my first round of work before she did.

"Are you ready for our break yet?" I asked her.

She looked glum as she replied, "I've got at least another fifteen minutes to knock these out. You go on without me."

"Come on. You can finish them after our break is over. Yeast donuts wait for no man, or woman, for that matter."

"If you're sure," she said as she pulled her hands out of the soapy water.

"I'm positive," I said.

We bundled up and headed outside. The wind had picked up, adding considerably to the chill that I'd experienced earlier. Spring was in the air, but it was easier to believe that at noon than it was in the middle of the night. Emma and I never let the weather stop us from our breaks, and we'd even shoveled snow from our seats on more than one occasion in the past to keep from missing our time together outside.

"So, how's your love life these days?" I asked her as a conversation starter.

"Actually, I met a new guy recently," she said.

"Is it serious?" I asked her.

"I thought that it might be at first, but I'm not going to go out with him anymore."

"That's fast, even for you," I said with a smile. "What was wrong with him?"

"He was just too nice for my taste, if you know what I mean," she admitted after a long pause.

"What? Since when was that ever a problem?" I asked her.

"The guy wouldn't argue with me about the little things, even when he was right. He'd just change the subject to avoid having a direct confrontation. It didn't take long before it started to drive me crazy."

I laughed. "That seems reasonable enough," I said, letting a hint of sarcasm leak through.

"I know it sounds petty, but it was really getting on my nerves."

"Hey, I'm not one to judge. At your age, you can afford to be as picky as you want to be. As you get older, though, some things might not seem as important to you as they are now. Believe me, I'm speaking from experience."

She frowned for a moment, and then she asked me, "Do you think I was too hard on him?"

"All I'm saying is that there are worse things in the world than being too nice," I answered. "It would be one thing if he was a doormat, but a little consideration can go a long way in my book."

"I don't know. I suppose that it wasn't that bad. He never backed down unless he didn't consider it important. Maybe I should give him another chance," she said uncertainly.

"Don't do it on my account," I said. I shouldn't have butted in, but it was hard not to give her my opinion sometimes, even when she wasn't asking for it. "How's school going?" Emma was taking classes at the community college with a plan of someday going away again to a university. She'd already tried it once, but she hadn't liked it, so she'd come back home, something that had been a great boon for me and my donut shop. I'd missed her, and having her with me again was awesome.

"Good," she said. "You know, it's school. What can I say? At least I get to sleep in my own bed at night."

I was happy that Emma was still close by. Sometimes I felt selfish about being happy that she was home again, but I couldn't help myself. Emma was so much more than just my assistant; her presence was something that I looked forward to every day she worked at Donut Hearts.

We were nearly ready to go back in when I saw a squad car go past. Chief Grant was driving, and he tapped his horn lightly as he passed us.

"What is he up to this early in the morning?" Emma asked.

"Jake and I called him before. No doubt he's been checking out the wagon factory since we left," I said.

Emma nodded. "From the sedate way he was driving, I'm guessing that he didn't find anything there."

"I can't help believing that whoever was there tonight was the person who killed Sully Jackson. I just wish I knew why." I had my own theories about the killer's motivation, but it was nothing I cared to share with Emma.

My assistant hesitated, and then she finally said, "Dad might have a few ideas about that."

I was starving for information about the murder, but I knew in my heart that the line that was between us shouldn't be crossed from either side. "Emma, you shouldn't tell me anything your dad wouldn't want you to. Our information blockade is a two-way street."

"I don't see how it matters. He can't print any of his theories, and goodness knows he has enough of them."

"Are you positive that he wouldn't mind you sharing them with me?" I asked her.

Emma was about to reply when the timer went off. The yeast dough was ready for more attention, and it wouldn't wait.

"You're right," my assistant said as we both stood. "I'm sorry I said anything."

"No worries. It's already forgotten," I said as I hugged her briefly. I was curious about what Emma's father thought about the case, but not enough to get into a quid pro quo situation with his daughter. "Come on. Let's get back to work."

The rest of the morning's prep work seemed to fly by, and before I knew it, it was time to open the donut shop for our first customers of the day.

I'd been expecting to see at least one familiar face when I walked out front to open the shop—like the mayor's, or even the police chief's—but the man I saw standing outside surprised me.

It was Jim Burr, one of my suspects, and from the look of his lowered head and drooping shoulders, he was sporting quite a hangover from his bender the night before.

The question was why was he at the donut shop so bright

and early the next morning when clearly the only place he wanted to be was back home in bed?

Chapter 12

"Good morning," I said quite a bit louder and cheerier than was called for when I opened the door for the electrician. "How are you?"

He held his temples as he tried his best to smile. "Take one guess."

"If you're here for a bit of the hair of the dog that bit you, I should warn you, none of my donuts have any alcohol in them."

Jim shuddered a little as I closed the door behind him and flipped the sign to show the world that we were open for business. When he spoke, his words were careful and measured. "I drank way too much last night. I think I'm going to go on the wagon after what happened. How bad was I?"

"Well, for one thing, you seemed pretty sure that Shirley Edam killed your boss," I said. "Did you have any particular real reason to suspect it was true? I mean now that you're sober."

He started to nod, but then he clearly must have thought better of the idea. "I might have been drunk, but that doesn't necessarily mean that I was wrong."

"Do you have any proof?"

Jim shook his head, a movement that he clearly regretted instantly. Through clenched teeth, he said, "Sully wasn't going through with the merger, no matter what she's been telling everyone. He told me himself yesterday morning that when he saw Shirley's reaction to his personal rejection, he didn't want to be in business with her."

"She claims that his rejection was no big deal," I said as I poured him a large cup of steaming black coffee. He took it from me immediately and drank greedily, despite its temperature.

"She would say that though, wouldn't she?" he asked.

"What nobody realizes is that Sully was her last hope. When he turned her down, she got really desperate."

The statement surprised me. "I'm sorry, but I don't buy it. There are plenty of other eligible men in April Springs alone," I said.

"I'm not referring to his dating rejection of her; I'm talking about her electrical contracting business. I hear things, being in the trade, you know?" Jim stopped to take another large gulp of his coffee, and I grabbed the pot so I could give him a quick refill. He deserved at least that much for coming by this morning in spite of the way he clearly felt.

"Such as?"

"From what I've heard, she's been gambling in Union Square," he said. "And she's been losing, big. Without Sully to prop her business up, she's going under, and it's going to happen fast."

"I take it you don't have any proof of this, though."

Jim Burr shrugged slightly, being careful not to move his shoulders too much. "The guy who told me this isn't the type to stand up and swear to it in court, you know? It's true enough, though. You can take it to the bank."

If that were indeed the case, it would provide Shirley Edam with a more powerful motive than personal rejection. The question was how could we confirm it? "How about your partner, Bob Greene? Can he at least vouch for your source as well?"

"Let's just leave Bob out of this, okay?" Jim asked.

That surprised me. I'd been under the impression that the two men did everything in lockstep. "Are you having some kind of problem with Bob?"

"No, but just because we work together doesn't mean that we're twins, you know what I mean? I do plenty of stuff without him, and he does the same without me."

"That still doesn't mean that I shouldn't speak with him again. Who knows what he's heard on his own?"

"You could always try, I guess, but not right now."

"Why not? Is there an issue?"

"No, it's just that he's getting ready to leave town and take a little vacation," Jim said. "But don't tell him that I'm the one who told you about it. He's leaving town tonight, so if you want to talk to him, I'd suggest you do it before he leaves."

"How long is he going to be gone?" I asked him.

Jim shook his head slightly. "I have no idea. He wouldn't tell me. For all I know, he could be gone for a month, or he might not ever come back."

"Can he afford to do that?" I asked him. "You two couldn't have made that much working for Sully."

"You'd be surprised. He paid us both well, and we've each been saving our money for years," Jim said evasively. Why didn't I believe him? I knew for a fact that those extravagant new cowboy boots he was wearing hadn't been cheap. I'd had a customer come in with a similar pair the year before, and he'd been bragging about just how much he'd paid for them.

"I like your boots. They couldn't have been cheap."

He stared down at them, and then kind of shrugged. "I got them on sale."

"I highly doubt that. They were custom made for your feet, weren't they?" I suddenly began to wonder what kind of vehicle he'd driven to the donut shop in. Was I missing something here?

"What are you implying, Suzanne?"

"Jim, where did the money really come from?" I asked him softly, but the question seemed to annoy him more than it should have.

"I told you. We've been saving up. So what if I splurged a little on a new pair of boots? It's not that big a deal."

"If you say so, but is that going to stand up after someone takes a peek at your bank account?" I asked him.

"You can't do that. You don't have the authority." He was afraid of something; that much was clear.

"I may not be able to, but the police won't have any problem accessing your records," I said. "It will make it easier for you if you come clean with me right now before they discover it on their own."

He wanted to tell me something. I could see it in his eyes. After a moment, though, he dismissed the urge. "I'm not going to get into that with you. I just wanted to drop by and say that I was sorry."

"You don't have anything to apologize for, at least not to me," I said.

Jim shoved a twenty into my hands, along with the nearly empty mug. "Thanks for the coffee. It was exactly what I needed."

As he started to leave Donut Hearts, I said, "Let me get you your change."

"Keep it," he said as he fled the donut shop as fast as he could.

I watched as he hurried down the street, but I couldn't see where he'd parked whatever he'd been driving. As I grabbed my jacket to follow him, I called out, "Emma, you've got the front."

"What's going on?" she asked as she stepped out of the kitchen, drying her hands on a dish towel.

"I'll tell you later," I said as I bolted out the door.

I was too late, though.

By the time I got outside, he was already gone.

I stuffed the twenty into the till as I wondered about Jim's behavior. What had brought him to the donut shop the first thing in the morning, particularly when he clearly had such a massive hangover? Why was it so important for him to speak with me so early? While he'd been there, he had done his best to reinforce the belief that Shirley had killed Sully, but was it sincere, or had he done it simply to deflect our attention away from him? And what about Bob? Had the two men had a falling out? I needed to speak with Sully's other employee before he escaped town, and I had to tell Jake about what had happened the second I saw him. I wasn't going to wake him up, though. He'd had a long night, directly because of me, so if he could sleep in, I wasn't about to take that from him.

Jim's visit had left me with more questions than answers, but for the moment, there was nothing I could do about it. After all, I still had a donut shop to run.

"Good morning, ladies," I said as the three women in my book club came into Donut Hearts at the appointed hour. Once long ago, they'd stumbled into the shop looking for a place to hold their meetings, and they'd quickly welcomed me into their group. I'd nearly forgotten about today's meeting, but fortunately I'd read the book on our honeymoon while Jake had been snoozing from eating too much fine food.

"How was your trip?" Jennifer, the stylish redhead of the gang of elegantly dressed women, asked me with a smile.

"Did you eat anything fantastic while you were there? Of course you did. After all, you were in Paris," Hazel said, a woman who seemed to constantly be on a diet for one occasion or another.

"Paris is Jenkins Bole's favorite city, you know," Elizabeth added. He happened to be the author of the book we'd be discussing in a few minutes, and she couldn't wait to drop his name into our conversation. "He told me so himself." Elizabeth lived to correspond with authors, and for the ones who actually responded to her inquiries, she claimed them as dear friends, regardless of the level of contact they ultimately shared.

"And why wouldn't it be?" I asked with a smile as I distributed coffee to each member of the group. "Before we get started, does anyone want a treat?"

"I really shouldn't," Hazel said as she studied the display case filled with goodies.

"Come on. You know you want to," Jennifer said. "I myself would love an elephant's ear."

"Is there any chance that you'd split one with me, Jenn?" Hazel asked tentatively.

"No, ma'am, I would not. Get one of your own. This one's going to be all for me," Jennifer said with a smile. I knew that she didn't eat like that all of the time. With her trim figure, she couldn't, unless she had one of those sickeningly fast metabolisms that burned the calories up as fast as she could consume them.

"I'll split one with you," Elizabeth volunteered.

"Are you sure?" I asked as I got out two of the massive confectionary treats. "You can each have one if you'd like."

"We're positive," they said in near unison. After I sliced the massive donut in half and plated them, I grabbed a few blueberry donut holes for myself.

"Is that honestly all that you're having?" Hazel asked, looking guilty about her choice.

"Don't forget. I'm around this stuff all day," I said. "Believe me, I do plenty of sampling in back."

"Then let's get started, shall we?" Jennifer asked as we took our seats.

I'd cordoned off our favorite couch and chairs earlier in honor of the meeting, and after we'd each sampled our treats and sipped our coffee, Jennifer dove right in. "I personally loved the way the author used auditory imagery throughout the book."

"What imagery are you talking about?" Elizabeth asked, clearly confused by her statement.

"Wasn't it clear to everyone else, too? I'm talking about his use of repetitive sounds throughout the book."

I'd noticed it too, but I wasn't going to comment on it, since I didn't want Elizabeth to feel as though she'd been the only one who'd missed it.

"Like what, for example?" she asked Jennifer.

"First, there was the doorbell that rang when he got the letter from his wife saying that she was leaving him, and then there was the programmed bell that rang on his cellphone when the police called to tell him that she was dead. A little later, we hear the church bell ringing during her funeral, and then the final bell comes from outside the courtroom after he is convicted of her murder."

"Those were just one long string of coincidences," Elizabeth said.

"I don't think so. They were too perfectly connected to be mere happenstance," Jennifer said as she looked at the rest of us. "Didn't anyone else see it, too?"

Hazel shook her head, and Jennifer looked as though she was beginning to doubt the conclusion that she'd drawn. It was time for me to speak up. "I thought I saw a connection there as well. It was rather striking, as a matter of fact."

"I'm sorry, but they aren't related," Elizabeth said firmly.

"How can you say that?" Hazel asked. "It seems clear now once it's been pointed out to me."

Elizabeth looked smug as she spoke. "I initially had the same question myself, but when I asked the author, Jenkins said that he had no intention of tying them together like that, and that if anyone did, it was in the reader's imagination, not the writer's."

"My question is, is the author always the best person to ask?" Jennifer inquired softly.

Elizabeth appeared to be outraged by the suggestion. "Of course he is. He literally wrote the book himself. If anyone would know what he meant, it would be him."

"Maybe he wasn't aware that he was doing it at the time," I offered. "I know sometimes my subconscious does things that I'm not entirely privy to."

That opinion, which I myself believed, was not popular among my fellow members. The two polar opposite arguments were that either the author was aware exactly of what he was doing the entire time, or that it was all pure coincidence. I didn't care enough to argue my point, and as the discussion continued to deteriorate, Jennifer quickly stepped in. "Let's move on, shall we? Who else was surprised by the twist at the end? I'm sure that was planned, and I must say, I feel that the author handled it like a master."

That appeared to mollify Elizabeth, who had taken Jennifer's earlier comments too personally. "He really is quite good, isn't he?"

"I loved this book," I said. "It's a shame it's the last one in the series."

"What makes you say that?" Hazel asked.

"I looked it up online. His publisher is dropping him. They said that while he did fairly well, and he always made them a profit, in the end he just didn't sell enough books to appease their accountants."

"That's ridiculous, isn't it? Just because they are shortsighted doesn't mean that the series is going to end, though," Elizabeth said, looking remarkably like the cat that swallowed the proverbial canary.

"Do you know something we don't?" I asked her.

"Jenkins has decided to continue the series on his own. He shared the news with me last night."

She made it sound as though he'd whispered the news into her ear across a candlelit dinner instead of via email over the Internet.

"So then, he's going to publish it himself?" Jennifer asked.

"Why shouldn't he? Lots of writers are turning their backs on their publishers and striking out on their own these days," Elizabeth said. "I personally think it's quite courageous of them, myself, and I applaud their gumption."

"I do, too," Jennifer said, taking the wind out of Elizabeth's sails. "After all, why should we be deprived of more books that we love just because a publisher happens to be wrong?"

"At least we're in agreement there," I said. "What does it matter who publishes our favorite authors? I just care about the books, and I'll read whatever my favorites publish, no matter how it gets to me. Elizabeth, did he give you any clues as to what the next one is going to be about?" I noticed that Hazel was frowning, so I quickly asked, "Do you disagree?"

"I know I'm alone in the group, but personally, I don't like e-books," she said softly.

"That's because you've never read one," Jennifer said. "They're wonderful."

"They can't ever replace the smell and the feel of my books. My real books," she added.

"Did you know that you can read them without your glasses?" Elizabeth asked.

"What? How is that possible?"

"You can adjust the type to any size you like," Jennifer said. "It's unbelievable how freeing that is. I don't have to hunt around for a pair of glasses to enjoy my book anymore, and I feel as though I've been freed from their tyranny forever."

"I don't know," Hazel said. "That might be nice, but I don't hold like holding some kind of device thingy in my hands. I would think it would get tiring after awhile."

"What gets tiring is holding up a seven-hundred page opus in hardcover," I said. "The great thing about reading electronically is that no matter how many pages an e-book is, it always weighs exactly the same."

"Hazel, if you just tried it, I know that you'd love it as much as we do," Elizabeth said. "By the way, to answer your earlier question, Suzanne, I think Jenkins is going to kill his publisher," she added with a grin.

"There's no need for anything that rash! He can just walk away and start over, can't he? I personally don't think violence is going to solve anything," Hazel said, the alarm clear in her voice.

"He's not going to do it in real life; he's going to bump the man off in print," Elizabeth said with a grin. "It sounds wondrous to me, and I'm going to be the first in line to buy it."

"I'm looking forward to reading that one myself," Jennifer said. "Now, let's get back to the book at hand. I thought the dog barking in the middle of the night was significant, but I never dreamed that would be what ultimately led to him getting caught."

We finished our discussion, our coffee, and our treats, and I had to fight off all three women from paying me. I loved their company, so I was glad to forego the meager profits I would have received from them. We'd agreed to take turns hosting the club at my donut shop, with one of us picking up the tab. Today had been my turn, and I wasn't about to let anyone take that privilege from me. "It's my turn, and that's the end of it," I finally told them.

After they reluctantly agreed, I asked, "So, what's our next title?"

"I'll email you all with it tomorrow," Jennifer said. We also took turns choosing our books, but it was common practice to tell the group about the next month's offering at the conclusion of every meeting.

"That's not fair," Hazel said. "I want to pick a copy up on the way home."

"Sorry, but the bookstore's not going to have it," Jennifer said.

"Then how are we going to read it?" she asked curiously.

"Go on. Quit dancing around and just give it to her," Jennifer told Elizabeth, and she reached into her oversized purse and handed Hazel a nicely wrapped box.

"What's this? It's not my birthday."

"Just open it," Jennifer insisted as she winked at me. I was as much in the dark as Hazel was.

"It's an e-reader," Elizabeth blurted out before Hazel could even finish unwrapping it.

"Okay," she said skeptically as she finished pulling off the bright paper.

"Tell you what," Jennifer said. "You and I will take it back to your house, and I'll show you how to use it. If you don't love it after half an hour, I'll take it back and we'll never bring it up again. What do you say to that?"

"I suppose it wouldn't hurt to try it," she said reluctantly as she studied it.

Twenty-seven minutes later, Jennifer called me at the donut shop.

Once Hazel had seen the wonders of her new device,

Jennifer hadn't been able to get the reader out of her hands, and we had one more convert to the fold.

A half hour later, I had another visitor come by my shop, a customer who clearly had more in mind than just buying a donut, or even discussing the latest mystery.

Something told me that this was going to be trouble.

Chapter 13

"That was quite a scene last night, wasn't it?" Shirley Edam asked as she approached the counter. "I'm glad your husband stepped in before things got even uglier."

"Would you have really hit Jim with that wrench?" I asked her.

"If it had come to that, I had every right to defend myself," she said brusquely, and I had no doubt that she would have done it. "I'd like two dozen donuts and four coffees for my work crew."

Funny, she'd never bought them donuts from my shop before, so I had to wonder if there was some other reason for her being there. Was she trying to justify what had happened the night before, or was she possibly fishing to find out what Jim might have told us as Jake had escorted him back to Stella's car? "Are there any flavors in particular you'd like?" I asked her as I grabbed a pair of folded boxes.

"It's your call. Mix them up for me."

I gave her a good selection, and as my back was turned to her, she casually mentioned, "I can't believe how drunk Jim Burr was last night. He was spouting quite a bit of nonsense, wasn't he?"

"You mean when he accused you of murder?" I asked without turning.

"Suzanne, you know that was just a drunken man's rant, don't you? I didn't kill Sully."

I decided not to address my thoughts on that possibility. Instead, I said, "He seemed pretty sure of it, didn't he?"

"Does that mean that you actually believed him?" she asked me, clearly incredulous that I might have taken what Jim had said to heart.

"Shirley, I'm not ready to make an informed decision yet. After all, we're still gathering facts. It would be nice if you could have someone corroborate your alibi."

"I'm sorry I can't snap my fingers and produce a credible witness," she said sharply. "Suzanne, I'm honestly a bit surprised by your attitude. After all, we're both women trying to run small businesses. We should stick together."

"I'm all for hiring you the next time I need any electrical work done here at the shop," I said as I started on the second box, "but that's where my loyalty to my gender ends. Murder is an equal-opportunity act, and I know from experience that women are just as capable of committing it as men are." I hadn't appreciated her playing the 'women in business' card. In my mind, it demeaned what we both did. If my donuts, or her electrical service, couldn't stand up against competitors—both male and female—I didn't want anyone frequenting my business solely because I was a woman; I wanted their business based on the treats I sold.

The first round of donuts had included some of our customer favorites, but this batch would be comprised mostly of our slow sellers for the day. After all, I was sure she wasn't really there for my treats anyway. Spending a little money was obviously her way of buying some of my time, not my goodies.

"So, you do think I killed him," she said resolutely.

"Shirley, I didn't come anywhere close to saying that," I replied as I finished loading the second box. I turned, stacked them on the counter, and then started getting the coffees she'd ordered. "All I said was that you weren't going to get a free pass from me just because you're a woman."

Shirley wasn't quite sure how to take that. "You're an odd bird, aren't you?"

I laughed. "I don't know if you meant that as a compliment or not, but that's the nicest thing you could say to me. I enjoy being different."

She shook her head as she handed me a twenty. As I added it to the till, I asked, "Are you going to offer Bob and Jim jobs on your crew after what happened last night?"

"I suppose that I might have done it despite what happened, but it's a moot point now. They've both essentially already told me they aren't interested in coming to work for me."

"What are they going to do? Are they striking out on their own?" I asked.

"I doubt it. Neither one of them has that kind of drive. Jim won't return my calls, so I got the message loud and clear from him, and from what I've heard, Bob is leaving town, and he's not even sure he's coming back. It doesn't matter. The more I think about it, the truth is that I'm not all that interested in having either one of them on my payroll."

As I handed her the small amount of change left after her purchase, I offered, "Would you like a hand with that?"

"No, I've got it," she said as she stacked the tray holding the coffees on top of the boxes and walked out with the entire load in one trip.

"What was that all about?" Emma asked as she joined me up front soon after the electrical contractor left.

"Shirley Edam was here trying to pry some information out of me," I said with a smile.

"What did she end up getting?" Emma asked.

"Two dozen donuts, twelve of which were our poorest sellers, and four coffees," I said with a grin.

"But no information?"

"Nothing that she wanted to hear," I said.

"Suzanne, I've been thinking that you should hear what my dad is up to."

I wasn't sure that I was ready to hear it, though. "Emma, we've worked really hard at keeping our private lives separate from our time together here. Maybe we should keep it that way, you know?"

My assistant frowned before she spoke again. "Even if it might help your investigation?"

"Even then," I said. It was tempting to hear what Ray Blake might have uncovered, but then again, I wasn't ready to share what Jake and I had discovered with him, so in the end, it was probably better if we didn't share anything.

"Okay," she said with a troubled smile. "If you're sure."

"I'm positive. How are things coming in back?"

"I'm just about caught up with this round of dirty dishes," she said as she grabbed two empty trays and a bin full of dirty cups and plates from the folks who had chosen to eat at the donut shop.

"That's the great thing about this place. There's always something else to do."

"I'm not complaining; the time goes by quicker when I'm busy," she replied as she disappeared into the kitchen again.

"I've filled your order, now what can I get for your friend?" I asked a customer who'd just bought a glazed donut and a glass of chocolate milk. His companion was one of the biggest stuffed animals I'd ever seen in my life, a soft and fluffy dog that was completely taking up one of my stools.

"He's not having anything. I'm returning him after I eat," the man said glumly. He was somewhere in his mid-thirties, and he'd looked a little ridiculous carrying the stuffed animal into Donut Hearts. There had to be a story that went along with it, and I was dying to hear what it might be.

"What's the matter? Did you two have a falling out?" I asked him with a slight smile.

"The fact of the matter is that I bought him for my girlfriend," he said glumly. "I even gave him a name, but she wasn't interested."

I had to know. "What did you call him?"

"What else? I named him Barkley," he said with a wry grin.

"That's kind of cute," I said as I rubbed Barkley's head from across the counter. "Why didn't she like him?"

"She said that he was too big, that she was a grown woman who deserved a more thoughtful gift on her birthday than a stuffed animal, and that I needed to get a clue, whatever that might mean," he recited.

"Do you mind if I ask you how old your girlfriend is?"

"She just turned thirty. Why?"

"No reason," I said, doing my best not to grin.

"You're judging me, aren't you?" he asked after taking a bite of donut. "Don't bother denying it. I can see it in your eyes."

"Well, you have to admit that it is an unusual present to give a grown woman on her birthday," I said.

"What's wrong with doing it?" he asked as he looked at his companion. "She has a stuffed animal on her bed, for goodness' sake. I thought Barkley would be a big hit."

"Let me guess. Is the one she owns now from her childhood?"

"Yeah, it's a little bear she got from her folks when she was a kid. His name's Mr. Bear, if you can believe that. Don't tell me that Barkley is a ridiculous name."

I smiled, but I did my best to make it as innocent as I could manage. "I have a feeling that Mr. Bear has more to do with the time she got him than the fact that he's a stuffed animal," I said. "Have you ever been to Two Cows and A Moose by any chance?"

"The newsstand? I saw it on the way over here. I live in Union Square, so I'm not really all that familiar with April Springs. Talk about your odd names, why would anyone call a business that?"

"The owner named the newsstand after her three favorite stuffed animals she had when she was a little girl," I explained. "In fact, if you swing by there after you leave here, you'll see that they are currently dressed up in karate outfits."

He drank some of his milk before speaking again. "If I live to be a thousand, I'll never understand women."

"If it's any consolation, we don't always understand ourselves," I said.

After he finished eating, he left me a dollar tip. "So tell me, what should I have gotten her instead of Barkley? And don't say a dozen donuts," he added with a grin.

At least he had a sense of humor about it. "That depends. Does she like jewelry?"

"She doesn't wear any that I've ever noticed," he said.

"How about a favorite scent?"

"No, she's allergic to perfume," he said. "See why I've been having such a problem thinking of a gift for her? I really love her, but it's impossible coming up with a present for her. She's special, and she deserves the best. I just don't always manage to make it clear how I feel about her."

"Candy?"

"No way. That would make her furious. She's always on a diet," he said.

"Does she at least like to eat out?" I asked him.

"She loves it. Italian is her favorite."

"I take it you've tried Napoli's," I said.

"She loves the place," he admitted. "We go there every Tuesday. I guess that I just wanted to do something special for her birthday."

I had a thought. "Hang on a second. Let me make a call." I dialed Angelica DeAngelis's private number. She owned Napoli's, and ran it along with her daughters. "Hey, Angelica."

"Suzanne Hart! When are we going to see you and that handsome new husband of yours?"

"Soon, I promise. Listen, I need a favor."

"For you? Name it," she said. We'd become close over the years, and I thought of Angelica as a second mother, and a dear friend.

"I have a customer who wants to do something special for his girlfriend's birthday."

"When is it?" she asked me.

"Hang on. I'll ask." I covered the phone and asked him. He looked miserable as he admitted, "It's today."

I shook my head as I got back on the line. "Today. Sorry, I know it's not much notice, but Napoli's is her favorite place in the world to eat."

"Have him bring her by at seven tonight," Angelica said. "I'll reserve our best table for them, Maria will personally wait on them, and I'll create a special menu just for them, including dessert. It will be a night she'll long remember."

"You're a lifesaver. Thanks."

"Come see me soon," she said.

After we hung up, I said, "You're all set. Be there at seven. Angelica's going to take extra special care of you and your girlfriend. It's going to be a real celebration."

The man looked stunned. "Why would you do that for me? You don't even know me."

"Maybe not, but Barkley vouched for you, so I know you're a good guy," I said with a grin.

He laughed. "I don't know what to say, but thank you."

"That works perfectly. Have a lovely time tonight."

"We will," he said. He collected his stuffed dog, and the two of them walked out together.

I kind of hoped he'd keep him, but I knew that the odds were against it.

"Suzanne Hart," Carl Descent said as he came into the donut shop ten minutes before we were due to close.

"Mr. Descent," I said. "What can I do for you?" Having the donut shop was turning out to be a real bonus to my murder investigations. After all, my suspects were parading in to see me, saving me the trouble of tracking them down myself.

"I understand my name came up in a discussion you were having yesterday."

How could he possibly know that Gabby Williams had mentioned him to me? I knew that April Springs was a small town, but this was crazy.

"I'm sure I don't know what you're talking about," I said.

He laughed, but there was no joy in it. "Perhaps I was mistaken." It was clear from his tone of voice that he didn't believe me, but I had him in my shop, and I wasn't about to waste the opportunity to grill him a little. Before I could ask him a question, though, he studied the racks of donuts behind me that we had left for sale. "How much would it cost me to buy everything that's left?"

I glanced at the racks, came up with a fair amount, and then

I doubled it. "Forty dollars should cover it," I said with a straight face.

Without batting an eye, he peeled two twenties off a roll of bills in his pocket and put them on the counter. "Box them up."

If he was trying to get on my good side by cleaning out my inventory, it wouldn't work, but I wasn't about to let him know that. As I worked at emptying my shelves and boxing the remaining donuts, I said, "I understand you really wanted to buy the wagon factory."

"That's true enough. The place has sentimental meaning to me," he said, "but your mother beat me fair and square."

"Why are you so attached to it?" I asked him, curious about his admission.

"My grandfather worked there long ago in the late twenties as a bookkeeper," he admitted. "I always thought I'd own the structure someday myself, and I thought I'd gotten it when your mother outplayed me at the last second."

"It doesn't sound as though you took losing all that well," I replied as I jammed the remaining donuts into boxes.

He shrugged and did his best to smile. "I lost sight of a basic fact. There's no room in business for sentimentality."

"I couldn't disagree with you more. There's a special place in my heart for Donut Hearts, and I wouldn't part with it for the world."

He shook his head, and this time his smile was legitimate. "You're a great deal like your mother, but I have to wonder, if someone came in and offered you a million dollars for the place, would you be cashing the check before the ink on it was even dry?"

"I don't guess I'll know until the situation arises. Is that a serious offer?" I asked him.

"Why, would you take it if it were?"

I had to think about it, but I'd meant what I'd said. "Like I told you before, Donut Hearts is not for sale, at any price," I replied as I finished boxing up his donuts. "Have you been by the factory since Momma started renovating it?"

"How could I have done that? That would be trespassing, wouldn't it?"

"Someone didn't seem to mind that fact," I said. "I found a stranger prowling around the place in the middle of the night less than twelve hours ago."

"Why are you telling me this?" he asked.

"I'm just making conversation," I said. "You look a little sleep deprived," I added with a twist.

"I need only five hours of rest per night, no more and no less. Otherwise, it's just wasted time that I could spend working," he said.

Wow, I really didn't agree with him about that. I stacked the three boxes of donuts up on the counter. "There you go. Thanks for your business."

He nodded, but made no move to collect them. "You should know that I didn't have anything to do with what happened to that subcontractor."

"His name was Sully Jackson," I said.

Descent nodded. "I didn't even know the man all that well."

"Maybe not before he wrecked your deal, but I have a hunch that you knew him afterwards. I understand that his recommendation to sell the building to my mother was pivotal in the owner's decision."

Descent actually laughed at my suggestion. "I'm fairly certain that the real factor was the piece of property your mother included in her cash offer. Mr. Jackson's endorsement provided an excellent smokescreen to disguise the seller's real rationale. Trust me, I had no reason to harm Mr. Jackson."

"Well, someone killed him, and I'm determined to find out who did it."

He looked amused by my statement. "How do you plan on doing that?"

"I don't know if you've heard the town gossip or not, but I've solved more than one murder in the past. This time, I even have a secret weapon."

"What's that?"

"My husband is a former state police investigator, and he's working on the case with me. Believe me when I tell you that whoever killed Sully is going to pay for it."

"Good for you," he said lightly. "Just don't try to involve me in it, and we won't have any problems."

"How could we, if you're telling the truth?" I asked.

"That's just it. You can't," he said, and then he turned and headed for the door.

"Don't forget your donuts," I called out, smiling.

"I don't want them anymore," he answered. "I'm sure I wouldn't know what to do with them."

"Sorry, but all sales are final," I replied with a smile.

"Do with them as you wish, then," he answered in kind.

Carl Descent was not the most cordial of men, but that didn't necessarily mean that he was a murderer. Some folks accused my mother of being abrupt, and even manipulative at times. She claimed they were traits that helped her in her business dealings, and I didn't doubt that Carl acted the same way.

That still didn't change the fact that he belonged on my list, and not because of what I'd heard from Gabby about him.

If he didn't have anything to hide, why had he gone out of his way to come by the donut shop and ask me if I was investigating him?

The man could stand a closer look, and I was going to make sure that Jake and I took one as soon as we got the chance.

Chapter 14

"Hey, Suzanne. I've got some things to share with you about our investigation," Jake said as he walked in a few minutes after Carl Descent left the shop. He scanned the empty trays behind me and added, "Is everything gone already? I was hoping to get something to nibble on." The disappointment in his voice made me smile. It was as though I'd caught a glimpse of him as he must have been when he'd been a boy.

I flipped open the boxes of donuts and other goodies between us. "Help yourself."

"I figured these were already set aside for someone."

"They were. One of my customers paid for them, but then he changed his mind about taking them with him."

"Is he crazy?" Jake asked as he reached in and pulled out a plain glazed donut. "These things are worth their weight in gold."

"I don't think he really wanted my treats in the first place, so I didn't push him too hard about taking the donuts with him when he left."

"Who are we talking about here, Suzanne?"

"Carl Descent."

"He was here? What did he want?" Jake asked after he swallowed another bite. "By the way, do you happen to have any more coffee?"

"I'll get you some," I said. After I brought him up to date on what had been happening at the donut shop and all of the visitors that I'd had, I said, "And that's about it. You said that you had news yourself. What did you find out?"

"Well, first off, I got a call from Chief Grant," he told me.

"Don't tell me that he was actually in the mood to share some of his information with you," I said as I poured some coffee for myself.

"The truth is that I think he felt bad about kicking us out of the wagon factory last night," Jake said. "I didn't ask about him about his motivation."

"So, what did he tell you?"

"First off, he wanted to bring me up to date about the boot print we found at the factory."

"You're the one who found it," I corrected him.

"We were investigating together," he said. "As far as I'm concerned, we share the credit."

"As long as we share the blame, too," I answered with a smile.

"You know it."

"So, tell me about the boot print?"

"Evidently it was brand new. The measurements indicate that it was a ten in men's or a woman's twelve in that particular style."

"Can't he tell which? It would helpful if we at least knew if our killer was a man or a woman," I said.

"Suzanne, we can't even be positive that whoever we spooked last night actually killed Sully. We shouldn't jump to any conclusions at this point."

"Well, I can see all of our suspects wearing work boots but Carl Descent. Should we take his name off our list? I've met the man, and I doubt that he's ever worn work boots in his life."

"Which could be why he'd wear them last night," Jake said. "If he was trying to throw us off his trail, what better way to do it than by implicating all of the other suspects."

This was getting frustrating. A clue that I'd considered to be important was quickly turning out to be pretty worthless. "How about our suspects? Did the chief have any idea what size shoes they wear?"

"It could have been any one of them, even Shirley," Jake admitted. "Their sizes are all about the same."

"Could that be why he shared the information with you in the first place? It doesn't cost him a thing to tell you that our lead was worthless."

"That's taking a pretty cynical point of view," Jake said. "I prefer to think that he's trying to make amends for evicting us."

"Okay, if it helps, then let's look at things that way."

Jake glanced around the empty donut shop. "Since you're officially sold out of donuts, what are the chances you could close the place up early?"

I thought about it for a moment before I spoke. "I don't see any reason why we shouldn't." I called out to the back. "Emma, if you'll do these last two trays, we can get out of here early."

"Sounds like a plan to me," she said as she came out of the kitchen, and then she noticed Jake standing there. "Hey there. I didn't hear you come in."

Jake smiled at her. "You know me. I'm stealthy."

She laughed. "Sure you are."

After Emma disappeared in back, Jake looked at me. "You think I'm sneaky, don't you?"

I kissed him. "That's exactly how I'd describe you. If you give me a minute, I'll run the reports on the register and make out the deposit for the bank."

"Could any of that wait until later?" he asked me. "There's something I've been dying to check out."

"You could have gone on and done it without me, you know," I said a little hesitantly.

"What, and spoil all of the fun for you? What if I find what I'm looking for? How would I feel about excluding you?"

"I'm glad you feel that way," I said. "I still have to run the report, but if we can lock the deposit up in your truck's glove box, we can put off the bank trip until later."

"You've got a deal," he said, and without even being asked, he started cleaning tables and flipping chairs.

"You know, sometimes you can be pretty handy to have around," I told him as I counted the money in the till.

"What can I say? I want to be sure you keep me," he replied as he grabbed a broom and started sweeping.

"No worries there," I said. As I continued to count the money, I noticed one twenty-dollar bill that was much older than the others. Had I ever had one that dated in my donut shop? I couldn't be sure. Instead of the overblown portrait of Jackson that I'd grown accustomed to and the sweeping blues, greens, and golds of our standard currency, this bill looked stark in its simplicity. The United States of America was written on a scroll, and Jackson's picture was downright tiny compared to its modern counterpart. I pulled out one of the newer twenties and noticed other differences as well. Instead of the Federal Reserve emblem, there was a large seven on it. The serial numbers were in different places as well. Even the picture of the White House on back was different. Someone had been digging deep to find that bill!

"Something wrong?" Jake asked. I looked up and saw him studying me.

"No, it's nothing," I said as I put the bill back in the stack. I could be easily distracted at times, but there wasn't time today. I had a mission.

The report checked out, and I jammed the bills, coins, and receipts—along with the deposit slip—into the bag I always used for my bank deposits and zipped it shut. "How are you doing?" I asked him.

"What do you think?" he asked proudly as he gestured around the front area.

"It looks good," I said. "All in all, you did a fine job. I think I'll keep you."

"That would be much appreciated," Jake said as he put the broom away.

Emma came out of the back, pulling her apron off as she walked. "Everything's all set in the kitchen for tomorrow." She spied the two mostly full boxes still on the counter. "Hey, are you going to be taking those with you?"

"Why, do you have a use for them?" I asked.

"I thought if we had any donuts left, I might take them to class with me," she said. "The professor loves your treats. Who knows? If I take him these, I might just get an A."

"You're going to use our donuts as a bribe?" I asked her with a smile.

"Hey, if it works, how bad could it be?" she replied with a grin. We both glanced at Jake at the same time and saw that he was frowning. "I'm just kidding," she said.

"About the bribe, or taking the donuts with you?" he asked her.

"If you want them, they are all yours," Emma said.

"No, you'd better take them after all. If they're with us, I'll probably just end up eating them." He slapped his tummy, which still looked plenty firm to me. "I've been really packing on the pounds since I left my job."

"It's amazing you can still even fit into your pants," I said as I kissed him. "What have you gained, a pound since our honeymoon?"

"A pound and a half," he reported, clearly displeased by the fact. "I suppose we could start running in the afternoons after you get off."

"Not unless you find a way to get a bear to chase me," I answered.

"So, should I take the donuts or not?" Emma asked.

"Take them with our blessing," I told her.

The three of us walked out together, and after Emma was gone, Jake said, "She really was kidding about bribing her teacher, wasn't she?"

"Jake, Emma is getting straight A's without any help from my confectionary treats. She's actually too smart to be working here with me."

"I don't know about that," he said as we made our way toward his truck. "She gets to spend all morning with you every day. In my book, that makes her one of the smartest people I know."

"Keep talking. Flattery will get you anywhere."

"I wouldn't say it if it weren't true," Jake answered. "Let me have your deposit, and I'll put it where it will be safe."

"Are you sure it will be okay in there?" I asked as he stowed it away in the glove box. I'd lost a couple of deposits before over the years, and it had always hurt.

"This truck was made back when they still used steel," he

said. "Nobody's going to bust into it and take your money."

"Okay, I believe you," I said. As he drove us to the wagon factory, I asked him, "What else did you do this morning besides talk to the chief? I know that you didn't sleep in." Jake was notorious about getting up early every day, even when he wasn't working. I wouldn't doubt that Emma and I were the only people he knew who got up earlier than he did on a regular basis.

"I spent most of it on the phone," he said. From his tone of voice, I could tell that he'd been frustrated by the experience.

"Who were you talking to?"

He frowned a little as he told me, "I was trying to use some of my old contacts to get us information on our suspects that might be useful to our investigation."

"From your voice, I'm guessing you didn't have much luck."

"I barely got the chance to ask! My old boss has put the squeeze on everyone I ever worked with at the state police headquarters. No one wants to cross him, and I can't really blame any of them for that. Suzanne, I was hoping that my connections might help us, but it appears that we're on our own from now on. I'm going to be worthless."

"You're kidding, right? Your experience and insights are much more important than any contacts you might have with the department. Jake, you're a trained and seasoned professional investigator. I'm a donutmaker. Don't you think that you bring our qualifications up a little just by being on my side?"

"Sure, I can see how you might look at it that way," he said dismissively.

"Trust me, it's massive," I said as he pulled up into the parking lot. Apparently we were going to start our investigation that day back where it had started, at the old wagon factory.

There was just one problem, though.

Officer Griffin was back on the scene, standing guard once again.

Chapter 15

"What's going on?" Jake asked the young officer as we got out of the truck and approached the deputy. "Does this mean that we can't go in?"

"No one's allowed inside, but the chief has given me a particular set of orders about you two," he said with a frown.

Oh, great. It appeared that we were going to be thwarted yet again.

Griffin surprised me though, when he suddenly grinned. "You two have the golden ticket, so you can go on in."

"What? Seriously?" I asked him.

"Scout's honor. You and your husband have been given all-access passes." Officer Griffin stepped aside, and Jake smiled at him as we walked inside the building.

"What do you think about that?" I asked him as the door closed soundly behind us.

"I think we'd better take advantage of the situation while we can," he said.

"Fine. Where should we start, at the scene of the crime?"

"We can check that out again later, but there's something else I want to look at more carefully first." My husband mounted the stairs two at a time, and I had a difficult time keeping up with him.

"Hey, wait for me. What's so urgent about getting upstairs?"

"I have a theory about those crates," he said, "and I'm dying to see if I'm right."

"You don't even have a pry bar on you," I said.

He stopped long enough to reach into his jacket and pull out a small pry bar less than six inches long. "Surprise."

"Do you honestly think that's going to be enough to get inside those old crates?"

"We're about to find out, aren't we?" he asked as we got to the room we'd been in earlier that day.

It turned out that Jake hadn't needed the bar after all. The crates were already open, and as a matter of fact, they were empty as well.

"Chief Grant, it's Jake," he said after he pulled out his phone and hit speed dial. After he did that, he put the phone on speaker before the police chief could answer so he wouldn't know that I was listening, too.

"What's up, Jake? I don't have a lot of time. I'm dealing with something right now."

"Is it about the murder?" my husband asked him.

"No, I'm investigating a robbery at the storage center over on Elm. Apparently someone broke into three units."

That piqued my husband's interest. "Was anything of value taken?"

"At this point, that's still to be determined," the chief answered abruptly. "So if you don't mind, I'd appreciate it if you'd make it dance."

It was odd hearing someone else giving Jake orders, but if he took offense, I couldn't hear it in his voice. "I'll make this quick, then. Did you open those crates on the second floor this morning, by any chance?"

"I did," he said.

"Is there any chance that you would be willing to tell me what you found?"

I could hear the chief hesitate, and then finally, he said, "I don't see what it would hurt telling you. Rivets. Lots and lots of rivets."

"What? I'm sorry, but I didn't quite catch that."

"I said they were full of rivets. I had one of my men bag and tag them just in case, but they were just plain old-timey rivets."

Jake nodded. "Got it. Thanks."

After he hung up, I said, "Sorry. I know that you're disappointed."

"Hey, it was worth a shot," Jake said as he idly tried to kick one of the crates, missed, and ended up scuffing the wooden floor instead.

I did my best not to laugh.

But then an odd thing happened.

Jake kicked the floor again, this time clearly on purpose.

Chapter 16

"Are you okay?" I asked him as he suddenly got down on his hands and knees. "Should I call for an ambulance?"

"I'm fine," Jake said as he studied the floor carefully.

"Come on. You missed that crate twice, and then you hit the floor. That is not anyone's definition of fine."

He looked up at me and smiled. "I admit that the first miss was an accident, but the second one was on purpose. Didn't you hear the difference in the floor when I kicked it?"

"It must have been too subtle for me," I admitted. "What exactly are you hoping to find?"

"Hang on a second and I'll tell you." He then took a pocketknife from his pants pocket and opened it. Using the largest blade, he started probing between the floorboards with it, sinking it all the way to the handle.

There was only one thing I could do; I got down on my hands and knees, too. If my husband was going crazy, then I was taking the trip with him. "Are you having any luck?"

"Not yet." He kept sliding the blade along the floor, and I was about to say something else when it evidently met with some resistance. "Now that's interesting," Jake said, and I could see part of the wooden floor lift a little as he probed the floor a little more. "What do you know? It's a secret cache," he explained as he pulled a section of boards up. They'd looked like a solid part of the flooring before, but now I could see that they'd been carefully disguised to look that way. Once the top panel was pulled off to one side, Jake and I looked down into the space to see what might have been hiding there.

The footprint of the opening was no bigger than the size of a standard sheet of paper, and about as deep as a loaf of bread. At first glance, I thought that the space was empty, but Jake reached into his jacket pocket and pulled out a small flashlight on his keychain and proved me wrong. I'd given it to him a year before for Christmas, and I always loved seeing it with his keys.

When he flashed the light down into the dark opening, I saw something that gave me pause.

It wasn't empty after all.

It looked as though there was money down there.

Not much of it, though. Jake reached in with his hand wrapped in a clean handkerchief and pulled out three bills, all of them twenties.

Only they weren't the familiar offset and oversized Jackson portrait looking back at me when I examined them.

They were all bills featuring the smaller version, just like the one I had outside in my deposit bag.

As Jake played the light more carefully into the hiding place, he said, "I'm guessing that there was quite a bit more here, and recently, too."

"How can you tell?"

"The top boards didn't make a perfect seal," he explained. "See that line of dust around the edges? The pattern should be uniform throughout the cache, but the entire middle of the area is clean."

"I see it," I said as I stood. "Hang on a minute. I'll be right back."

"Suzanne, where are you going?"

"There's something I need to show you," I said. "Let me have your truck keys."

Jake clearly wanted more of an explanation—I could see it in his glance—but he handed them over without commenting. "While you're gone, I'm calling the chief. He needs to see this, too. I've got a hunch that the corner of that torn bill we found in Sully's hand is going to match these. Whoever took the money probably killed him."

"You do that," I said as I left the room. Downstairs, I saw Officer Griffin still standing watch. "If I go out, can I come back in again?"

He grinned. "The Chief didn't mention a limit on your number of visits, so be my guest."

I got to the truck, and I didn't realize that I'd been holding my breath until I opened the glove box and saw my deposit bag still sitting inside safely.

Was the bill still there, though?

I riffled through the money searching for the bill that I'd taken in that day, but the first time through, I couldn't find it. Frantically, I did a more methodical search, and sure enough, there it was! I considered wrapping it in a tissue, but I'd already handled the thing at least twice, so there was no doubt in my mind that my prints were already on it. I pulled a twenty out of my wallet, the lone one I had, and stuck it into the bag with the rest of the deposit. I had a hunch that there was no way that particular bill was ever going to make it into the bank. I wasn't pleased about the prospect of losing twenty bucks, but if it helped our investigation, I'd have gladly donated ten times that to the cause.

After the truck was secure again, I made my way back to the building's front door.

"That was quick," Griffin said with a smile.

"What can I say? I'm efficient," I replied with a grin of my own.

Jake was just getting off the phone when I walked back into the small room upstairs. "What was so urgent that you needed to borrow my truck?" he asked me, clearly not able to contain his curiosity one second longer.

"Not your truck, just your keys," I said as I handed him the bill in my hand. Before he could protest that I hadn't mimicked his handling of the bills we'd found earlier, I said, "It was in with my deposit, so I've already handled it at least a couple of times."

"Maybe so, but I haven't," he said. "Hold it up for me, would you?"

I did as Jake asked, and after a quick study of the bill, he

said, "Put it down gently on the top of that crate, would
you?"

"It can't be a coincidence, can it?" I asked. "The day we
find three old twenties in the wagon factory, another one
shows up at my donut shop."

"Suzanne, these bills were all issued in 1928. They have to
be linked. Do you have any idea who paid you with that
particular twenty?"

"Sorry. I don't have a clue," I admitted. I hadn't been
observant enough at the time, and now it might cost us a
valuable clue.

"Don't beat yourself up about it," Jake said. "I've seen
your shop when you're busy, so I know how crazy it can be.
According to what you told me earlier, three of our four
suspects came by Donut Hearts today: Carl Descent, Jim
Burr, and Shirley Edam."

"Does that mean that Bob Greene is in the clear?"

"Not exactly, but he can at least go to the bottom of our
list."

Something had been nagging me all along, and I suddenly
realized what it was. I'd forgotten to tell Jake what Jim Burr
had said about his work buddy. "Jake, I forgot to tell you
something."

"What is it? Did Bob come by the shop, too?"

"No, but Jim told me that Bob was leaving town this
evening, and he might not be coming back. Shirley
confirmed that without prodding, too. How could Bob just
afford to walk away?"

"Maybe he's the one with the money," Jake suggested.

"Who has what money?" a voice asked us from the
doorway.

I looked over to see the chief of police standing there, but
he wasn't alone.

Momma and her husband, Phillip, were with him, too.

"Hey, Momma. What are you two doing here?" I asked.

"I own the building, don't I?" she replied. "The chief and I were discussing when it would be released when Jake called him. Chief Grant thought we should come along, since we have a vested interest in the investigation ourselves."

"Not me," Phillip said. "I have no desire to dig into this, or any other case, for that matter. The only thing I'm interested in these days is local history. After all, I'm the one who convinced your mother to restore this building in the first place."

I hadn't known that. Momma added, "It's a good investment, and besides, I hate to see the old landmarks torn down so unceremoniously, and that's exactly what Carl Descent was planning to do. What did you find?"

Jake offered the bills to the police chief. "We found three old twenties in a cache under the floor where the crates had been stacked," he said.

Chief Grant had a plastic bag ready for them, and Jake slid them inside as he went on to explain, "They're all from 1928."

That got Phillip's interest. "So, it's true," he said with a frown.

"What's true?" I asked.

"I've been coming across several references that the original owner of the factory, Martin Polly, hid a fortune in this building that no one could ever account for. He never trusted banks or the stock market, which turned out to be pretty savvy, given that the Great Depression occurred just a year after these bills were printed. The thing is that I was certain that his cache was in gold, not paper money."

"Three bills doesn't exactly make a fortune," the chief said.

"There was a great deal more down here than that, and recently, too," Jake explained as he showed the police chief what he was talking about.

"Why is this bill over here by itself?" Momma asked as she started to reach down and retrieve the bill I'd placed on one of the crates.

"Don't touch that!" I said a little too loudly in such a confined space.

Momma jerked back her hand as though she'd been reaching for a snake. "Why on earth not? What's wrong with it?"

"Nothing, but it might be evidence," I said in a much calmer voice. "Someone paid me at the donut shop today with it, and it's a match with the others we found up here."

"They're counterfeit?" Momma asked. "Who would fake a batch of old bills?"

"It's not as crazy as it sounds," Phillip said. "Think about it. There weren't any of the modern security measures in the old bills like the holograms and embedded strips we have now."

"True," the new chief said, "but these are legitimate, at least as far as I can see." He looked over at me and asked, "Suzanne, I don't suppose you remember who gave you this one, do you?"

"Sorry, I don't, but I think I can narrow it down to one of three people. Shirley Edam, Carl Descent, and Jim Burr all came by the donut shop today, and every last one of them paid me with at least one twenty."

The chief looked disappointed, and who could blame him? It would have been nice to be able to narrow our search even a little bit at that point. Chief Grant took out another evidence bag and carefully placed the bill I'd taken in a bag of its own. "We'll dust it for prints anyway," he said. "Thanks for calling."

"Is that it?" I asked.

"What else can I do?" Chief Grant asked me. "Suzanne, Sully's murder is a priority for me, but I'm trying to run an entire department, too. As much as I'd like to, I can't spend every waking moment worrying about one case, even if it is murder. There's just too much on my plate as it is right now."

"I understand," I said, and I did. I'd never given my new stepfather enough credit when he'd had that job, and I wasn't about to repeat the mistake with my friend. In my mind, it was even more reason for Jake and me to dig into the case.

For us, it would be our only priority.

"I still don't understand why you found paper money in that cache," Phillip said. "I need to go back to the library and do more research."

"I'll drop you off on my way, dear," my mother told him. Before she left, she kissed my cheek. "Come see me later, Suzanne."

"Why? Is anything up?" I asked her, concerned by her summons.

"Isn't it enough that I miss my daughter?" she asked, and I realized that I'd been spending so much time with Jake since I'd been back that I'd neglected her, and Grace as well. I'd have to make more of a conscious effort not to let my new married life interfere with the two women in the world who meant the most to me.

"I promise," I said.

"Good. Phillip, are you ready to go?"

He'd been conferring with Chief Grant and Jake about something, but he quickly broke away from them. "Bye, all."

The chief said, "Hang on a second. I'll walk you out." When we didn't follow, he asked, "Was there something else you two needed to see here?"

"We might hang back and look around a little more," Jake said, "if that's okay with you."

Chief Grant grinned, showing his youth for a moment. "Are you kidding? I'll take all of the help I can get. Thanks, I mean that for both of you."

"We're happy to do it," I said. It was good to see a flash of my old friend, even if it was brief. The weight of being temporary police chief was impacting him, and I wondered if he'd be able to stand up to the added strain of the job at his young age. He was smart, and he was tough, but I couldn't help worrying about him. After all, that was what I did with the people in my life that I cared about.

"What exactly are we looking for?" I asked Jake after everyone else had gone. "Do you really think there's more money hidden around here somewhere?"

"This isn't a treasure hunt, Suzanne. I'm looking for clues."

"Sure, but if we stumble across a fortune along the way, we're not going to just ignore it, are we? It sounds as though it might add up to be a great deal of money."

"I've got a hunch that the rumors are just that, rumors, plain and simple. I've learned over the years that there's more phantom gold than has ever been mined in the history of the world. Besides, what would you do if you found a fortune? You wouldn't retire from Donut Hearts, and don't try to tell me that you would."

"I'm not so sure about that. Sleeping in until seven sounds like a little bit of paradise to me right now."

"You'd get bored within a month of retiring," he said.

"How could you possible know that? Are you?" I asked, turning the topic to one a great deal more serious than our previous idle speculation.

"Not a chance. Being married to you is anything but boring, and besides, who's retired? Here I am, working on a murder case, just like always. The only differences are that this time I'm doing it for free, and I have no official status."

"The upside is that you get to work with your wife, though," I said with a grin.

"Believe me, that makes up for the difficulties, and then some," he said as started investigating the flooring in one of the other rooms upstairs.

"If we're not looking for treasure, then why are we trying to find new caches?" I asked him.

"Suzanne, we saw someone prowling around up here this morning with a flashlight. What if their presence wasn't related to the money we found earlier? They could have been here looking for something else that had been hidden away earlier, something that might give us a clue about the identity of the killer."

"That's something that I never considered," I admitted.

"That's why there are two of us," he answered with a grin.

We spent the next few hours kicking, tapping, and probing the upstairs floorboards, but we didn't have any luck finding any other secret caches, or anything else, for that matter.

Whatever wealth had been taken out of the old wagon factory was apparently all that there had been, at least as far as we could see.

Chapter 17

"What should we do next?" I asked Jake as we headed down the stairs. It looked as though someone had tried to clean the central wagon wheel emblem in the floor, but I could swear that I saw a hint of something remaining now that the temporary plastic sheeting had been removed. No matter how much they cleaned, sanded, or even replaced the wood and stones inlaid in the floor, I knew that I'd probably always see it there. My stomach rumbled a little as if on cue.

"I know you're hungry," Jake said. "I am, too, but can it wait half an hour?"

"I think I can stand going without food for that long," I said with a smile. "What did you have in mind?"

"I'd like to look around the murder scene while we have it to ourselves, and then we'll grab a bite to eat before we look for Bob Greene."

"Okay by me," I said as we reached the center emblem. "What exactly are we looking for?"

"Anything that we might have missed before," he said. "The chief is going to release the building soon, and I want to have one last look around before he does."

I felt a slight shiver as we approached the exact spot where we'd found Sully the day before. Had it been just twenty-four hours since he'd been murdered right under our noses? A part of me was still in shock from the event, but I'd learned early on that life goes on. There was nothing we could do to bring Sully back, but at least we could do our best to catch his killer.

Jake looked around intently, but I honestly didn't have a clue what he hoped to see. After all, the police had examined the crime scene thoroughly, no doubt photographing it from every angle as well, and then we'd studied it ourselves. Besides the torn fragment of the twenty-dollar bill—which was beginning to look more and more significant—no one had been able to come up with anything useful, at least as far as we were aware. I decided to widen my focus a little and started walking around the room in broadening circles to see if there was anything outside of Jake's narrow scope of interest.

"What are you doing?" he asked me.

I glanced over and saw that my husband had been watching me. "The same thing you are. I'm trying to make sure that we didn't miss anything."

"Good. Keep it up," Jake said, and then he went back to his close examination of the exact spot where the murder had occurred. How long could he keep analyzing the same few square feet? I didn't see anything out of the ordinary during my own search, and after a few minutes, I decided to get a breath of fresh air. I didn't want to go out the front door since Officer Griffin was still posted there, so I headed for the back; it was the same avenue the killer had used to make their escape, as well as whoever had visited the wagon factory the night before, which more than likely was the same person.

I had my hand on the doorknob when something caught my eye. Squatting down to get a better look at it, I could see that it was a torn piece of flannel sporting a partial red-and-black-check pattern.

I'd seen that same pattern on Sully's shirt, as well as Bob and Jim's tops. Even Shirley Edam's robe had sported a similar design.

It appeared that we were on the right track after all.

"Jake, I need you over here," I said without disturbing the cloth.

"Hang on one second," he said absently. "I think I might be onto something."

"This is important!"

That got his attention. As he walked over to me, I saw that he was frowning. "What is it, Suzanne? I had the inkling of an idea, but now it's gone."

I pointed to the torn cloth. "This counts more than a fleeting thought. Look at this. I know for a fact that it wasn't here yesterday."

Jake knelt down and studied the fragment without touching it, either. After he took a few photographs of its location with his cellphone, he said, "I'm fairly certain that it wasn't there, either. Whoever left this behind must have done it last night when we spooked them."

"I don't know who did the actual spooking," I said. "All we have to do now is find the shirt this tear matches, and we could have our killer."

"Or not," Jake said as he pulled out a plastic baggy and placed the cloth inside.

"Since when did you start carrying evidence bags on you?"

"Since I started digging into murder with you," he said. "These aren't official. I just grabbed a few baggies from our pantry at home." I loved when he called our cottage home.

"Why don't you think it will help?" I asked.

"Suzanne, chances are that whoever tore their shirt knew it and disposed of it. I'm guessing that we'll never find the original garment this matched."

"Maybe not, but at the very least, it eliminates Descent from our equation, don't you think?"

"What if he has a red-checked flannel shirt, too?" Jake asked.

"What are the odds of that? Sully and his men wore them as a kind of a uniform, and just because Shirley's bathrobe pattern matched last night, that doesn't mean that her closet's full of them, too. At least that much could have been a coincidence."

"So, you think that either Bob or Jim killed Sully?"

I shook my head. "I'm not willing to go that far, but they do both deserve closer looks. I just wish we could get into their closets and have a look around."

Jake looked at me carefully. "Suzanne, I'm not breaking into anyone's apartment, do you understand that?"

"Relax, Jake. I wasn't suggesting it," I said.

"Really, because that's what it sounded like to me."

"There must be another way to do it without breaking the law," I said.

"First, we have to find Bob Greene," Jake said. "I know we're both hungry, but if we stop to eat, we might miss him."

"I can go without food as long as you can," I said. My stomach betrayed me by rumbling at that moment. "Pay no attention to that," I added with a grin.

"Don't worry. We'll eat soon enough," he said as we headed back to the front.

Officer Griffin was pulling down the last of the crime scene tape as we walked out.

"Is the building officially being released now?" Jake asked him.

"Yes, sir," he replied. Though Jake was no longer an officer of the law, he still commanded the respect he deserved.

"Like I said before, just call me Jake, Happy. Do you happen to know where your boss is at the moment?"

"I sure do. He's at the Boxcar," Officer Griffin volunteered.

"Thanks," Jake said.

As we got into his truck, I said, "I thought we were going to look for Bob before we ate, not that I'm complaining, mind you."

"We are, but we need to bring Grant up to date on what we've found first. We can't conduct searches, but he can. Who knows? Maybe we'll get lucky and one of our suspects neglected to get rid of that torn shirt."

"Only if they were drunk," I said.

"Well, wouldn't they both qualify as being inebriated last night?" Jake asked as he drove us to the diner.

"Bob was a little tipsy, but I'm starting to have second thoughts about Jim's true condition," I said.

"Why do you say that? I thought Jim Burr was the one who looked the drunkest between the two of them."

"There's something I've been wondering about. It almost felt as though it was all just an act. When we found them at the bar, Jim seemed to be hammered, and when we got to Shirley's, he kept acting as though he was under the influence, but I'm beginning to wonder whether he was ever really that drunk, or was he just putting a show on for our benefit?"

"That hadn't occurred to me, but I suppose that it's possible," Jake said. "At this point, we really can't know one way or the other. The real question is if you're right, what would it serve him for us to believe that he was drunk?"

"Maybe he was hiding something, or it's even possible that his attack on Shirley's character was part of his scheme all along, and he wanted to be stone sober in order to sell it. Honestly, I'm not exactly sure yet, but I'll keep thinking about it and I'll get back to you."

"You do that," Jake said with a grin.

When we got to the diner, the police chief's squad car was there, but it wasn't empty.

Acting Police Chief Stephen Grant was in the front seat, arguing with someone on the passenger side, and it only took me a moment to realize it was Grace.

What was this about?

When they spotted us, they stopped talking instantly and Grace opened her door.

Chief Grant said, "Grace, hang on one second. I said I was sorry."

"I heard you the first time," she said primly, "but I'm still not sure that I believe you."

"Is that why you're still angry with me?" he asked her.

"Boy, they sure picked the right man to be the new police chief, didn't they? You're quite the detective, aren't you?"

As Grace marched quickly toward us, I asked her softly, "Are you okay?"

"I'm fine," she said softly as she gave me a secret wink,

and then she stopped and turned to her boyfriend, who was five steps behind her. "On the other hand, the chief has a serious need to get his priorities in order."

"I can't just drop whatever I'm doing whenever you call. This is important." The moment the words were out of his mouth, he realized that he'd made a mistake. "Not that you aren't," he added quickly, but it was too late.

Grace's smile could have cut diamonds. "Understood. Thanks for clearing that up."

She kept walking, past the diner and through the park where we both had shortcuts to our homes.

"Are you honestly going to go after her?" I asked Chief Grant as he started in her direction.

"Suzanne, what choice do I have? I've got to make her see reason," he said.

"Would you care for some free advice, worth exactly what it's going to cost you?" I asked him gently.

"Maybe later," the chief said. "I need to make her see that she's being completely unreasonable about this."

"Good luck with that," I said, doing my best not to smile.

Jake stepped in front of him, effectively barring his way. "Stephen, it might not hurt to listen to what Suzanne has to say."

Chief Grant was about to step around him when he must have reconsidered. After a second of hesitation, he turned to me. "What is it you wanted to say to me?"

"Give her ten minutes to cool off before you go after her," I said. "If you press her right now, you might as well be arguing with a brick wall."

"I'd love to give her the time, but I've got a job to do," he said, his voice clearly deflated. "I didn't mean to forget our lunch date, but something came up. She keeps claiming that I don't make her my priority, but right now I just can't."

"Find a way to let her know how special she is to you," Jake said calmly. "If you let it, this job will eat you alive, and trust me, at the end of the day, you'll be old and alone with no one around who cares one bit whether you live or you die."

"Wow, that's pretty grim," Chief Grant said thoughtfully.

"It was meant to be. While you're waiting for a little time to pass before you try talking to Grace again, you really should look at this," he said as he pulled the torn piece of shirt from his pocket, now safely secured in a plastic bag.

"Where did you find this?" the chief asked, clearly back in his element.

"Don't give me the credit. Suzanne found it hooked on a nail by the back door. It wasn't there yesterday, so our best guess is that whoever's shirt it came off of was there last night when we showed up."

The chief took the fabric from Jake and studied it. "This black-and-red-check pattern seems to keep showing up, doesn't it?"

"That means that we're all on the same track," Jake said.

"But it still leaves us with at least two suspects," the chief said.

"Actually, we have three that like this pattern," I corrected him, and then we told him about Shirley's robe the night before.

"Three it is," the chief agreed, and then he looked off in the direction of where Grace had just left. "Is that enough time for her to cool down, do you think?"

I considered it, and then I said, "You still have a few minutes, just to play it safe. Why don't you stop by the flower shop and get her some yellow roses before you go over there?"

"Why not red ones?" he asked. I liked that he hadn't argued with me about the need to give her flowers at all. It was clear the man wanted to make amends for missing their lunch.

"She likes red just fine, but she's a sucker for yellow."

"Good tip," the chief said, and then he patted his shirt pocket where the fabric scrap now resided. "Thanks for turning this over to me, too."

"Oh, I almost forgot," Jake said as he pulled out his phone.

"I also took a few shots with my camera of where we found it."

"Send them to me, would you?" the chief asked.

"I'd be happy to."

After he was gone, Jake said, "Suzanne, that was nice of you to help him."

"I was doing it more for Grace than for Stephen," I admitted, "though I like him just fine, too."

"Either way, it was sweet."

I looked at the diner's front door, so close and yet so far away, and then I put on my bravest face. "Okay. Let's go find Bob Greene."

Jake laughed. "I don't suppose twenty minutes will hurt. Let's go on in and grab a bite first before we tackle him."

"Are you sure?"

"I'm positive. Neither one of us is going to be thinking clearly if we're both hungry. If we get two of Trish's lunch specials, we can be in and out before we know it."

It didn't turn out to be that way in the end, though.

Fate had other plans for us that afternoon.

Chapter 18

"Come join me," my stepfather said as he beckoned from a table near the back. I didn't see how there would be room for us, since the top was covered with what looked like faded old letters and ancient newspapers.

"Is there any room for us?" I asked him as we approached.

"No worries. I can stack this stuff up and make enough space for you both," he said as he began to do just that.

"What is all of this?" Jake asked as he looked down at the papers.

"Dot wants to commemorate the history of the wagon factory inside the space, and I think it's a great idea. She's had me going through old letters, newspaper clippings, that kind of thing ever since she bought the place. I've found the most fascinating things. For example," he said as he rustled through a few of the papers, "here's a sheet from the old factory payroll. Look at those wages."

I glanced at the paper and whistled.

Phillip grinned at me. "I know what you mean, but don't forget, things were a whole lot cheaper to buy back then, too."

"I know, but it's still interesting," I said. I could see how he might get hooked on digging into our local history.

"You're really enjoying your retirement, aren't you?" Jake asked him as we settled in.

"Are you kidding? I'm so busy it's hard to believe that I ever had time for work before. I've always been interested in local history, and now I have all of the time in the world to dig around in the dusty corners of April Springs."

"I'm glad you found something to keep you busy," I said as Trish approached. I turned to my good friend and said, "Two specials, please."

"The catch of the day is meatloaf, mashed potatoes with brown gravy, and green beans. I can tell you from first-hand experience that it's an excellent choice. Two teas as well?"

"That sounds great to me," Jake said as he studied one of the letters Phillip had collected.

Trish laughed as she looked at me. "It looks as though your husband is catching the bug now, too. Chief, can I get you anything else?"

"I told you to call me Phillip, Trish," he said.

"Sorry, but I just can't bring myself to do it. Once the chief, always the chief."

Phillip grinned, clearly pleased to keep the designation, even though he no longer held the job. "I could use more coffee whenever you get a chance, but there's no hurry at all."

"Coming right up," she said, and then she turned back to me. "I'll be back in two shakes with your food."

"We'll be here," I said. After she was gone, I started to ask Jake something when I saw the expression on his face. "Jake, what is it?"

"You're not going to believe this, but I just found something," he said as he pointed to the letter in his hands.

"You saw it, too? That's what I wanted to show you," Phillip said enthusiastically. "You read about the mention of gold at the factory, didn't you?"

"Is there really gold hidden somewhere in that old building?" I asked the men softly. The last thing I wanted to do was to encourage anyone else to visit the old wagon factory after dark looking to enhance their bank account.

"I don't know if it's *still* there, but it appears that there was a great deal of it at some point," Jake said. "Listen to this. It's from Martin Polly, the man who used to own the company." He read aloud, *"I don't trust banks. Never have, never will. I like to keep what's mine close. Besides, if I kept it with Harley in his vault, I wouldn't be able to take it out at night and let it dance through my fingers. It always amazes me how heavy gold coins really are. Paper money is fine for payroll, but I prefer something I can sink my teeth into. Evidently, other folks do, too. Someone broke into the*

*factory last night, and unless they had a sudden hankering
for a new buggy, they were looking for my secret stash. They
didn't find it, though, and they never will. I'm too smart for
them. What I have is safer than a locked steel door any day
of the week and twice on Sunday. Sticks and stones may
break my bones, but they also protect me and what's mine. If
someone did happen to stumble across it, I'd lose more
than…"*

Jake turned the letter over, but he frowned when he saw
that it was blank. "That's it?"

"I haven't found the rest of the letter yet," Phillip
explained, "but I'm not about to give up."

"Let me know when you track it down," Jake said.

"I didn't know you were interested in history, too," my
stepfather said.

"It's intriguing, but I'm more concerned with the present
right now. If there's still gold somewhere in that building, it
could give the killer plenty of motive."

"After all these years, do you honestly think there's a
chance that *any* gold is still on the premises?" I asked them
both.

"Why not?" Phillip asked. "Martin Polly died of a heart
attack in his sleep, and as far as I can tell, he never told
anyone where he'd hidden his gold. As far as I've been able
to determine, nobody's found it in all these years."

"What about the cash we found?" I asked Jake.

"That could have just been the paper money he kept for
payroll that he talked about in the letter," my husband said.
"It's beginning to seem as though there are *two* caches of
value there."

"And it's just been sitting there all these years waiting to be
discovered," I said.

"Maybe. Then again, it could all be gone now," Jake
replied. "If someone stumbled across it, it's not likely that
they'd broadcast the news."

"Well, we know for a fact that at least some of it was still
there until very recently," I said. I was about to add more

when Trish brought our food and drinks. I thanked her as she placed them in front of us. "I have a question for you."

"Shoot," she said.

"Have you gotten any odd-looking money as payment lately?"

"Do you mean counterfeit?" she asked me with a frown.

"No, it's perfectly legal currency. It's just old," I said. Trish looked surprised. "How did you know?"

"Are you saying that you got some, too?"

The diner owner reached into her apron and pulled out a pair of twenties from the same vintage as the one that I'd found in my own till. "Do yours look like these?"

"May I see those for one second?" Jake asked.

Trish handed them over. "They're still good, aren't they?"

"They are," Jake said as he studied the bills intently, forgetting all about his late lunch. After a moment, he dug out his wallet, and then he frowned. "Suzanne, I've got thirty bucks in my wallet, but I need ten more."

"Let me check to see if I have it," I said as I grabbed my own slim wallet.

Phillip beat me to it, though. "Here you go," he said as he handed Jake the money.

I found a five and five ones and handed them to Jake instead. "Thanks for the offer, but I've got this covered."

"It's no problem," he said as he tucked his offered money back into his pocket. Was there a slight look of pain in his eyes as he did it? I hadn't meant to hurt his feelings by refusing his money. It was something that I'd have to fix later.

Jake handed the money to Trish. "Mind if we swap?"

"I was going to keep them as conversation pieces," she said, "but if you'd like to have them, they're yours." After she scooped up the offered replacement money, she grinned. "In even trade, I mean."

"Do you happen to know where you got those?" I asked her.

"No, I didn't notice at the time. It wasn't until I was doing my totals at the end of the day yesterday that I spotted them."

"Do me a favor and start noticing," I said. "I'd love to know who's paying with old twenties."

"I can do that," Trish said. "Should I tackle them and hold them until you get here when it happens the next time?" Clearly the prospect pleased her more than it should have.

"Don't act like it's any big deal. Just give me a call if it happens again," I said.

"You've got it. Now eat up. Your food is getting cold."

"Yes, ma'am," I said with a grin.

Jake was still staring at the bills, though. "I don't get it."

"What's not to understand?" I asked, and then I took a bite of my food. The meatloaf was excellent. I cut off a small piece with my fork and then dragged it through my potatoes. Momma hadn't approved of the action when I'd been a kid, but I was a grown woman now, so I could eat however I wanted to. As far as I was concerned, it was one of the real privileges of being an adult.

"Whoever found this money is making no effort to hide it from the world," Jake said. "It's most likely stolen, and it's easily identifiable, so why not at least go to another town to pass the bills off?"

"I think you're giving the thief too much credit."

"Maybe so," he said as he absently took a bite. "Still, it seems pretty brash to me."

"That's because you're used to dealing with a higher class of bad guy," Phillip said as he looked up from the clipping he'd been reading. "On this level, they're a little easier to catch."

"I hope you're right," Jake said, "because so far, we're not having much luck."

"It's just a matter of time now," I said. "We're dealing with someone who's being sloppy about it, and that means that we'll catch them sooner or later."

"I vote for sooner," Jake said.

I stabbed a few green beans with my fork, and after I ate them, I asked, "Are we absolutely positive that whoever killed Sully is the same person who stole those twenties from the factory?"

"It's easier to believe that than the two events are mere coincidence, especially since Sully was holding the torn edge of one of the bills when we found him."

I frowned. "That's a good point."

"Something's bothering you, Suzanne. What is it?" Jake asked.

"If you killed someone for money, would you go around town on a spending spree afterwards, especially if the bills were so easy to spot?" I asked him. "You'd think that even the dumbest criminal would know not to draw attention to themselves."

"I think you're giving the killer too much credit," Phillip chimed in.

"Maybe so," I said, and then I took another bite of my lunch.

By the time we finished eating, I was in a much better position to go off in search of Bob Greene. We left my stepfather at the diner, content with his letters and clippings from the past. After we paid with the last of our cash, I asked Jake, "Do I have that to look forward to soon?"

"What are you talking about?" he asked.

"I'm just wondering. Now that you're retired, are you going to start collecting stamps or something?"

Jake laughed. "I used to love collecting coins as a kid, but you're safe for now. I resigned from the state police; I didn't retire. I'll find something to occupy my time before long. You're not worried about me, are you?"

"Always," I answered with a grin.

"For richer or for poorer, right?"

I hugged him tightly. "If you ask me, we're rich right now in every way that counts. Money is just icing on the cake. I don't care if you never get another paycheck in your life. I just don't want you to get bored."

"With you around? I'd say that was impossible," he said

with a grin. "Don't be concerned about me, Suzanne."

"If you say so," I said. "Now, do you have any idea about where we might find Bob?"

"If he's getting ready to go out of town, I have a hunch we'll be able to find him at his apartment, and I happened to look up the address this morning while you were busy making donuts."

"Then let's go have a chat with him, shall we?"

"Where are you heading off to in such a hurry?" Jake asked Bob Greene loudly as we approached him in his driveway. He was putting a box in his truck bed, and from the looks of it, he'd better be just about finished packing if he expected to get much more into it.

"You don't have to shout. I'm standing right here," he said. The man looked absolutely miserable, and Jake wasn't about to take it easy on him.

"Hung over, by any chance?" Jake asked loudly as he patted him on the back.

"Something like that," Bob said as he sat down heavily on the back of the tailgate and grabbed his temples.

"Funny, but your partner seems to hold his liquor a lot better than you do," Jake responded.

"That's because he only has one drink a day, no matter what. That's his rule. Me, I'm not that smart, especially when I lose somebody like Sully."

"Even yesterday?" I asked. I'd seen Jim Burr drink more than that myself, or had I? He'd been sipping one when we'd gotten to the bar, and he'd surely acted drunk standing on Shirley's front lawn, but was that all that it had been? This new information just made me feel that I'd come to the right conclusion about him after all.

"Even yesterday," Bob said.

"You never answered my question," Jake piped in, returning his voice to a more normal amplification. I had a feeling that if he started getting answers he didn't like, my husband's volume control would go up again. "Where are you rushing off to so soon after Sully was murdered?"

"I'm going to work for my uncle in Greenville," he said. "I wasn't leaving until tonight, but now I just want to get out of here."

"Why were you waiting around before?" I asked. It had been curious behavior, at least in my mind. When I wanted to go somewhere, I just went, and Bob struck me as being the same kind of person. So what had been keeping him?

"I was hoping to get paid what I had coming to me, but now that I know that isn't happening, I'm hitting the road."

"How were you planning to get money out of a dead man?" Jake asked.

"Haven't you heard the latest? Shirley's picking up all of our old clients, but she's not taking over the business like Jim and I had heard she was going to do. That means that she doesn't owe anyone Sully owed, but she gets all of the benefits of taking over his clients. I have to admit that it's pretty slick, even if I am the one getting shafted by it."

"Is that official?" I asked him.

Bob shrugged. "What's it matter what you call it? Sully's business is effectively gone, I'm leaving town, and I don't know what Jim's planning on doing, but I doubt that it's going into business for himself. Besides, he doesn't have to, the lucky dog."

"Why not?" I asked.

"Man, have you two managed to find out anything? He got a big inheritance from an uncle up in New York. Evidently he won't have to work unless he wants to, and I've got a hunch that he's not going to want to. I might have stuck around and tried to take over Sully's operation if Jim had shown the slightest interest, but he told me that he's putting his pliers down, and he's never going to pick them up again, so what am I going to do, go to work here for Shirley? I don't think so, even if she'd have me."

"Would that be so bad?" Jake asked him.

"Let's just say that I'd rather start over in a new city than try to make a clean start of it here in April Springs. This town is tapped out for me, and now that Sully is gone, there's nothing left here for me."

"I thought you and Jim were good friends," I said.

"I thought so, too, but evidently I was wrong. Now that he's got some cash, he's too busy for his old buddy." Bob stood up, winced a little, and shut his tailgate carefully. "That's the last of it. Whatever's left, the next guy can have."

I had one last question for him. "When we saw you at the bar, you were wearing a leather bomber's jacket. Was it new?"

"No way," Bob said. "It took me six months to save up for that thing, and then Jim up and buys a pair of custom cowboy boots on a whim that cost more than every stitch of clothing I own. It's just not right, if you ask me." He looked embarrassed as he turned to my husband. "You wouldn't happen to be able to spare a few bucks for gas, would you?" Bob asked Jake. "I wouldn't ask, but I'm not sure that I'll make it on what I've got in the tank."

Jake looked at me and I nodded. He reached into his wallet and pulled out four singles. "Sorry, but it's all I've got on me."

"It'll do fine," Bob said as he took the money. "Thanks for that."

"Don't mention it," Jake said.

Bob saluted us both with his index finger, and then he got into his truck and drove away, leaving his apartment door standing wide open.

"Is there any reason to search what he left behind?" I asked Jake.

"I can't imagine," my husband said. "Do you believe him?"

"I might not have until he asked us for money, and then he took those four bucks so gratefully. He's broke. There's no doubt in my mind. If he killed Sully, it wasn't out of greed."

"I don't think he did it at all," Jake said.

"Why do you say that?"

"If he's as poor as we think, he'd have waited until after payday to kill his boss, unless it was a crime of passion, and he just doesn't strike me as the type."

"Even though he's leaving town in the middle of our investigation?"

"There's that against him," Jake said. "We don't have to take him off our list entirely, but we can at least bump him to the back end."

"I can go along with that," I said. "Where does that leave us?"

"I'd like to talk to Jim and Shirley again," Jake admitted. "I wonder if we looked in Jim's wallet what we'd find."

"Like a batch of old twenties, for instance?" I asked.

"Exactly. Bob's jacket might have been old, but those cowboy boots we saw weren't cheap, and they were so new they might as well have been sporting a price tag. From everything we've heard, they must have cost him a fortune."

"Then let's go," I said. "Are you going to call the chief and bring him up to date on what we just learned?"

"I owe him that much, Suzanne. After all, he's letting us muck around in his case as much as we want to, and I'm not entirely sure that I'd be nearly as understanding if I were running things."

"Then let's just be glad that you aren't," I said with a smile. "Should we go looking for Shirley or Jim first?"

"I've got a hunch Shirley might be easier to find, so let's start with her," Jake said as he checked his watch. "She's probably in her office now."

"Then let's go there first. We can track Jim down after that. I'm glad you're working on this with me."

"Now that Grace has dropped out, I don't have much choice, do I?" he asked me with a grin as he drove toward the electrician's office.

"Is it that arduous a task for you to spend your afternoons with your brand-new bride?"

"No, but I can think of a few things I'd rather be doing with you than interviewing suspects and running down clues."

I patted his leg. "All in good time, my dear. For now, we need to focus on the task at hand."

Jake nodded in agreement. "Once we find Sully's killer, why don't you take a few days off and we can go somewhere?"

"We were just on our honeymoon not that long ago," I answered with a hint of laughter. "And now you're expecting me to take another vacation from the donut shop?"

"Hoping, not expecting," he replied with a grin.

"Let me see what I can work out with Emma and Sharon."

"That's all I'm saying," he said as he parked the truck in front of Shirley Edam's electrical business. We didn't even have to knock on the front door.

Shirley was already standing outside talking with Jim Burr, an odd situation considering all of the people in April Springs she might have been having a conversation with at that moment.

Chapter 19

"Is everything okay here?" Jake asked as we approached the two of them. At least they weren't yelling at each other this time, which was something.

"No worries, folks. Everything's fine," Shirley said.

"I just came by to apologize to her, face to face," Jim said contritely. "I was out of line last night, and I've been ducking her calls until I could come by and say it in person. I'm not afraid to admit it; when I'm wrong, I'm wrong."

"Yes, you were," Shirley replied. Wow, she wasn't cutting him any slack, even though he was clearly there with his hat in his hand. I glanced over at Jim, expecting him to be upset with her curt reply, but he just nodded in agreement.

"Anyway, that's all I came by to say, Shirley," he said. "I'll be seeing you around."

The electrical contractor took that in, and then she offered him her hand, which Jim took. "Listen, I know we haven't been on the best of terms lately, but I could always use a man of your skills on my team. What do you say? Do you have any interest in coming to work for me?"

"Thanks for the offer, but I'm getting out of the electrical business. With Sully dead, I've kind of lost my taste for it." It surprised me a little that he hadn't even hesitated in rejecting her offer.

Jim walked three steps away from us when Jake called out, "Suzanne and I would love to have another chat with you, if you've got the time."

"I'm heading over to the bank right now," he said with a frown. "And after that, I'm going to grab a bite to eat at the Boxcar. You're welcome to join me there if you'd like to."

"We'll catch up with you soon," Jake said.

"I was hoping to see you two today," Shirley said. "Do you have a second for me?"

"You bet," I said. "What's up?"

"I've been thinking about what you asked me earlier. I'd completely forgotten all about it, but I did speak with someone about the time Sully was being murdered."

That stopped Jim in his tracks, and he turned back to face us. "Who's vouching for you, Shirley?"

"Stanley Jacobs," she said. "I completely forgot that he dropped by to add something to the bid I was writing up for him. At the last second, he decided to add two more breakers to his garage panel, and he wanted me to figure it into his quote."

"And he'll be able to confirm the time of his visit if we ask him?" Jake asked.

"I don't see why not. There's just one hitch, though."

"What's that?" I asked.

"He's out of town for the next few weeks, but when he gets back from his cruise, I'm sure he'll confirm it," she said. "Anyway, that's all that I wanted to say. Was there any particular reason you two came over here?"

I couldn't exactly admit that we were there to grill her further, especially since she'd just found a way to clear her name. "No, we were just driving by, saw you talking to Jim, and we thought we'd pop in and see what was going on."

"You wanted to make sure there wasn't a repeat of last night, right?" Jim asked wryly. "Man, I've got to stop drinking. It's starting to be a real problem."

"You were upset about your boss," I said. "I get it."

"Yeah, Sully was one of a kind."

"Well, if you all will excuse me, I've got things to do inside," Shirley said.

"Mind if we stay out here a minute and chat?" Jake asked her. "We'd like to speak with Jim while we have the chance."

"I don't care what you do," she said, and then she disappeared inside. "As long as it doesn't involve me, we're good."

Jim glanced at his watch. "I really do need to go by the bank."

"Is it about your inheritance?" I asked, watching him carefully for some kind of reaction.

"You've been talking to Bob, haven't you?" he asked me warily. "He was the only one I told about it."

"He mentioned it," I admitted. "That must have been quite the windfall for you to just walk away from your career. Who exactly was it that left you the money?"

"You didn't know him. It was an uncle from New York," he said, "but I'd really rather word didn't get out. People start acting funny when they find out that you've come into a little money."

"What was his name?" Jake asked as he pulled out the same kind of notebook he'd used while he'd been a state police investigator.

"Why do you care?" Jim was edging up to open hostility at that point, and I wondered how hard Jake was going to push him.

"It's nothing personal. We're following up on every lead we get. Once we check him out, we'll be able to tell the police chief what we discovered, and you should be all set."

"Why would the chief need to know about my inheritance?" Jim asked.

Jake studied him a moment before he spoke. "Jim, we know for a fact that a great deal of money was stolen from the wagon factory recently. You've been working there, and now all of a sudden you have come into an inheritance from an uncle nobody in town ever knew existed. It all seems like a bit of a stretch, if you ask me."

"Are you saying that you don't believe me?" He was doing his best to act indignant, but it wasn't very convincing. What he appeared to be was scared. Jake had a way of asking questions that would shake any but the most seasoned criminal.

"I'm not saying that I have an opinion one way or the other at the moment about your guilt or innocence," Jake replied, though from his tone of voice, it was clear that he did. "All we need is his name and a way to contact whoever handled your uncle's estate, and then we'll leave you alone."

"I know my rights. I don't have to tell you anything," Jim said sharply, and then he started for his truck.

I decided to step in. "Jake, let me have one of those bills."

My husband frowned, but then he reluctantly handed me one of the old twenties—still in its own baggy—from his pocket. I held it up so that Jim could see it, but I made sure to keep a tight grip on it. "These bills are suddenly showing up all over April Springs. How long do you think it will be before we track one of them back to you? Wouldn't you feel better if you just came clean and told us the truth?"

At least he didn't deny it outright. "So what if I have some old bills? They're still legal money, aren't they?"

"They are, but every date on the twenties we've found so far is from 1928 and earlier."

"So? Maybe my uncle left me a lot of old money."

"Give it up, Jim," Jake said. "We know." His voice had an air of judgment to it that made me want to confess to something, and I hadn't done anything.

"Know what?" Jim asked haltingly.

"It's pretty clear that you were working by yourself at the factory and stumbled across the cache where the money was hidden. What happened? Were you running a new electrical line, and you had to access the floor there? It won't be too hard to get a confirmation of that. One look at the wiring blueprints will show exactly where the new line was supposed to go, and Bob should be able to tell us if you were running it alone or not. It's pretty clear that he didn't know about the money, so we have to assume that you didn't tell anyone about it, not even your partner. Sully found out somehow though, and he confronted you about your theft. Is that when you tore your shirt, when you ran out of the building? We found a fragment of it snagged on a nail, and I'm willing to bet that we can match it up to one of your shirts at home. You killed Sully to keep his mouth shut about the theft, but he managed to point one last finger at you before he died. The funny thing is that you're probably not even aware of it."

Jim's face was ashen now. It was pretty clear that Jake's assumptions were spot on. "I don't know what you're talking about," he said, his voice barely a whisper.

"Deny it all you want to, but the two of you must have struggled, and one of the bills was torn in the conflict. When we find the twenty that matches the edge we found near Sully's body, you're going away for murder."

"But I didn't kill him!" Jim protested. "I swear it."

"You weren't with Bob at the time of the murder, were you? How strong do you think your alibi's going to be when we tell your old partner that you found a cache of money and didn't share it with him?" Jake asked. "Do yourself a favor and admit it right here and now. You know that you want to." His voice softened a little as he added, "We know that you didn't mean to kill him. You panicked, and you did a very bad thing, but it wasn't planned."

Jim shook his head. "I didn't kill Sully," he said, his voice nearly filling with tears as he spoke. He was on the edge, ready to break, and Jake knew just where to apply the pressure.

So did I.

"You must feel awful about what happened, Jim. You and Sully were friends, and your argument with him was the last thing between you, wasn't it?" I asked him softly. "The evidence doesn't lie. We know that you're not a bad man deep down inside. You did something you shouldn't have, but you didn't plan on killing him. In a way, it was almost an accident that he found out what you'd done. What choice did you have when he confronted you about taking that money? Come on. Tell us what happened. You'll feel better to tell the truth."

Jim started to speak, and then he began to softly whimper. I reached out and patted his shoulder, and after a moment, he trusted himself to talk. "You're right. Sully saw me coming down the stairs with some of the money in my hands. When he confronted me, I lost it."

"So you killed him," I said softly.

"No! I never laid a hand on him! He grabbed one of the twenties out of my hand and it tore! Sully figured out where I'd gotten it, and he demanded that I turn it all over to your mother. Since she owned the building, it was rightfully hers. I told him that I would do what he asked, and he said that if I didn't, he'd tell her himself. I left to go get the money I'd taken earlier, I swear it, and the next thing I heard was that somebody had killed him before I could get back with the cash I'd grabbed! I might be a thief, but I'm not a murderer!"

"What happened? Did you push him away from you? The rebar could have already been there, and he fell against it. Nobody's going to think that you planned this ahead of time," I said softly.

"I keep telling you, I didn't do it," Jim said again, sobbing this time.

Jake nodded, pulled out his cellphone, and after a brief conversation, he hung up. Chief Grant was there within three minutes, and before we knew it, Jim Burr was cuffed and being pushed into the back of a squad car.

"Good work, you two," the police chief said to us as he closed the door.

"He kept saying that he didn't do it," I said.

"What would you expect him to say?" the chief asked. "Give him a little time. He'll confess soon enough." Then he turned to my husband. "Don't you think?"

"The odds are good," Jake said, nodding. "The man's clearly been feeling guilty about what he did, and when Suzanne and I pushed him, he cracked."

"Then that's that," the chief said. "By the way, I checked his wallet. It's jammed full of old twenties."

"He already admitted to being a thief," I protested. "But he claims that he's not a murderer."

"What did you expect him to say?" Chief Grant asked, and then he got into the car and drove Jim to the station.

I noticed that Shirley had been watching everything from inside, and a curtain closed quickly when I looked directly at her.

"Let's go home, Suzanne," Jake said.

"Do you really think it's over?"

"That's the way it looks to me," he said. "You were really good when you were talking to him. I was impressed. You did better than some seasoned cops I've seen during that interrogation."

"If you say so."

"You don't seem too happy about it," he said.

"I don't know. It just seemed too easy, you know?"

"Sometimes that's the way things turn out," Jake said. "Maybe now we can get back to some sense of normalcy around here."

"Whatever that means," I answered. For some reason, I still wasn't able to let things go. Most likely Jim had killed his boss by accident during their struggle, but what if he hadn't? A part of me wanted to believe him, but where did that leave me?

If I believed that someone else had killed Sully, it looked as though I was on my own.

As far as everyone else was concerned, the case was closed.

Chapter 20

Three days later, there was still no murder confession from Jim Burr, and the nagging suspicions in my mind became bolder and bolder.

Unfortunately, Jake wasn't inclined to agree with me, though.

"Suzanne, I wouldn't mind learning that Jim Burr had confessed to Sully's murder myself, but wishing it is not going to make it happen."

"He admitted to stealing the money, though. Why wouldn't he tell the entire truth?"

"Admitting to being a thief is a far cry easier than confessing to murder," Jake said. "I've seen it happen a few times myself."

"So, you honestly believe that he killed Sully?"

"Without any new evidence, I'm inclined to feel that way. The simplest answer is often the correct one."

"What about Shirley Edam's alibi?" I asked.

"What about it?"

"Didn't it seem awfully convenient to you that the one person who could attest to her location during the murder happens to be out of touch for the foreseeable future on a cruise? We're in the age of mass communication, and yet we can't make a simple telephone call to confirm her whereabouts."

"It happens," Jake said.

I was really getting frustrated with my husband's pat answers. "Jake, am I going crazy here?"

"Of course not," he said soothingly. "I understand the instinct not to let go of the case until there's a complete and satisfying resolution, but we really don't have much choice."

"We could press Shirley harder, and we could also go after Carl Descent more than we have so far. There's something suspicious about his behavior in all of this that I just don't like. He claimed to want to preserve the old building because of his grandfather, but other reports we got were that he was going to raze the structure to the ground as soon as all of the papers were signed. Something just doesn't add up."

"Is it possible that you're just being paranoid?" Jake asked me gently.

"Anything's possible, I suppose," I said. "I still want to do some more digging."

Jake sighed, and then he got up from the couch. "Fine by me. Where should we start?"

"Sit back down," I said with a smile. "You've been looking forward to that *Law and Order* marathon on television for days. Watch the good guys catch the bad guys."

"What are you going to do while I'm watching? I don't want you interviewing any suspects alone, even if I do think the case is over," Jake said.

"How about if I just do a little more digging into some of the background of the case? If I promise not to speak with any of our other suspects directly, will you watch your show and let me satisfy my own curiosity?"

"That depends. What did you have in mind?"

"First of all, I'd like to talk to Momma about the building sale," I said. "Somehow I believe everything hinges on that."

"I can understand you thinking that. It's not just the scene of the crime; it's also where the motivation for the murder was supplied."

"If Jim actually killed Sully," I amended.

"If," he agreed. "Are you sure that you don't want me to go with you?"

"Positive," I said. "Enjoy yourself. Crack open a soda, break out the chips, and have a blast."

The familiar bars of the *Law and Order* opening played, and as Jake glanced at the television screen, he said, "If you're sure that it's okay, I think I'll stay here."

"Just because we're married, it doesn't have to mean that we do everything together," I said as I kissed the top of his head. "I just want to snoop around a little to satisfy this nagging feeling I've been having in the pit of my gut." I glanced at the television. "Besides, I've already seen just about every episode of that show ever made."

"Okay, but call me if you need me," he said, already lost in the blooming storyline on television. I loved my husband, but he was clearly a man of limited interests. He had lived the life of a detective, and now he was experiencing it vicariously on television. I was going to have to find something meaningful for him to do before he got bored out of his mind with his situation, but that was going to have to wait.

Right now, I needed to talk to Momma.

"Suzanne, what a treat to see you so unexpectedly," Momma said, holding her phone to her chest as she opened her front door. "Come in. I'll just be one minute."

"Thanks," I said as I came in.

Momma nodded at me, and then she returned to her call. "Carl, I'm sorry, but it's not going to happen, no matter how generous your offer might be. No, not even a ghost is going to persuade me. Good-bye, Carl." After Momma hung up, she said, "I'll give the man credit; at least he's persistent."

"Is Descent still trying to buy the wagon factory from you, even after everything that's happened lately?"

"He is, but it's all in vain. I'm determined to see this rehab through to the end, no matter what. The factory is going to be a showplace for April Springs, and I'm going to be the one behind it. Now, to what do I owe the pleasure of your visit?"

"Do you have a second?"

"For you? Always," she answered. "Phillip is in the den poring over more papers from the wagon factory. He's convinced that there's gold hidden on the premises, no matter how much I try to dissuade him of the notion."

"How can you be so sure?" I asked.

"Oh, no, not you, too. Don't tell me you've caught the

gold fever yourself."

I shrugged. "The stories are all clear enough. Martin Polly didn't trust banks, or even paper money all that much. He must have done something with all of that gold."

"I'm sure that he spent it," Momma said, "Or at least his family did. I can't imagine that there'd be any place left in that old building that we haven't looked."

"Have you been actively trying to find it, yourself?" I asked her. My mother was a great many things, but trying to get rich quick didn't fit her profile at all.

"Of course not, but that doesn't mean that I haven't kept my eyes open during the renovation. We were able to recover a great deal of the cash Jim stole, and I consider that the only bonus we'll ever get from the project, not that it was an inconsiderable sum."

"How much cash did he find?" I asked.

"Jim confessed to finding thirty thousand dollars, and he admitted to spending a little under two of that, so all in all, it's not bad, though it's not exactly what I'd call a fortune."

"How was he planning to retire on twenty-eight thousand bucks?" I asked. "He'd be lucky if that lasted him a year, the way that he was spending it."

"I honestly don't believe that he was thinking that far ahead," Momma allowed.

"You missed *that* stash of cash," I pointed out. "How can you be so sure that there's not another hiding place somewhere else within the building?"

"You and Jake searched the second floor, and we've ripped up nearly every floorboard on the first floor. If it's there, where could it be?"

"I don't know, could it be squirreled away somewhere inside a wall?" I asked.

"Sorry, but we stripped the walls down to the studs so we could rewire and insulate the first and second floors."

"How about the attic?"

"We've been over every square inch of it. There was nothing there," she said confidently.

"The basement?" I asked, desperate to find an answer.

"There isn't one. Not even a crawl space," Momma answered. "I'm sorry, but there is no more treasure left in that building."

"Actually, it might be too soon to say that," Phillip said as he came into the room holding a faded letter in his hands. "I might have found something."

"What is it?" Momma asked.

"Listen to this. I found a copy of another letter from Martin Polly. *'The emblem of my company holds the only real value to my life. Beneath it is everything that matters to me, and I'll go to my grave knowing that keeping it safe is the noblest thing that I can do.'* What do you think of that? I'm not exactly sure what it means, but it's an odd way to phrase his beliefs, isn't it?"

"The man was proud of the company he built almost single-handedly," Momma said. "What's all that surprising about that?"

That's when I got it. "That's not it. What if the meaning of that passage is literal?"

"What, that the stones and timber used to create the seal in the floor are made of gold?"

"Hear me out," I said, suddenly getting excited by my new theory. "Who did he write that letter to, Phillip?"

"His wife, Enid," my stepfather supplied.

"When did he write it?"

"It was dated a month after the factory opened," he supplied. "She was visiting with her family in Los Angeles during her father's long illness. She wasn't on the scene the entire time that the factory was being built, and he kept a copy of every letter he wrote to her while she was away."

"What's your point, Suzanne?" my mother asked.

"Momma, you said yourself that you've explored just about every nook and cranny of the entire building. Let me ask you something. Did you ever disturb the wagon factory emblem in the course of everything that you've done so far?"

Momma frowned. "No, we wanted to leave it intact for

history's sake. Phillip, it was your idea. Suzanne, surely you don't think it's valuable."

"Other than as a window to the past? No, I don't think so. I've studied the stone and wood carefully. They're real enough."

"Then what do you mean?" Phillip asked, getting caught up in my enthusiasm.

"I'm not talking about the materials we can see," I said. "I'm referring to the space beneath them. We've already seen that Martin Polly liked secret hiding places. The cache of money proves that. What I'm wondering is if there's one more niche that we haven't uncovered yet."

"I don't know," Momma said. "It all seems rather farfetched to me."

"But it's possible, isn't it?" I asked.

"In order to find out," Phillip said, "we're going to have to tear up the last piece of floor that we've been trying to preserve."

"Not if we do it right. There must be some sort of catch or release hidden somewhere if there's a cache there. All we have to do is find it. Who wants to go with me?"

"I'll go," Phillip said eagerly.

I turned to my mother. "Momma? How about you?"

"I'm sorry, but I just put a cake in the oven, so I have to be here for at least another half an hour. Can it wait?"

"Tell you what," Phillip said. "Why don't Suzanne and I go check it out? If we find anything, we'll head straight back here and tell you all about it."

"Is that okay with you, Suzanne?" Momma asked. She'd been wanting me to spend more time with her husband, and I had to wonder if she wasn't using this as an excuse to make it happen.

"That's fine, if I can drive us in my Jeep," I said.

"It's a deal," Phillip said, and then he kissed his wife before he turned to me. "Let's go, Suzanne. This is exciting."

"It's probably going to turn out to be nothing," I said, trying to keep his enthusiasm at a healthy level.

"Maybe, but what if it's not?" he asked as we walked to my Jeep together and got in.

The drive to the factory was a short one, and no one was working, so we had the place to ourselves. I got down on my hands and knees and began to study the emblem buried within the pattern of the floor. Though the blood had dried thoroughly and had been washed away with repeated cleanings, I was still careful where I put my hand.

I didn't want to touch the spot where Sully Jackson had breathed his last breath.

"I don't see anything," I said as I started studying the inlaid wood and stone. "Do you?"

"There's got to be something here," Phillip said as he joined me. In random patterns, we both began pushing and probing the stone and timber at various spots, hoping to find some kind of trigger mechanism that opened it.

If there was anything there, we couldn't find it.

"Should we just tear up the floor?" Phillip asked me. "It's the only way we'll ever know if we were right or not."

"Hang on a second," I said as I spotted a small hole in the center of one of the timbers. "What's that?"

"It looks like a wormhole to me," he said.

"Do you have a pen on you?" I asked him.

Phillip retrieved one from his notebook and handed it to me. "It's too big. It's never going to fit."

"Not like this, but I have an idea," I said as I unscrewed it. While it was true that the pen itself wouldn't fit into the opening, the plastic cylinder that held the ink might. I pulled the pen apart and then pushed the plastic tube downward into the hole. It started to bend under the pressure, and I was about to pull it out, when I heard a distinct click.

Something had happened to the emblem as I'd done it.

As one piece, the entire thing shifted in the floor, raising itself up enough to reveal edges where I could pull it open.

As I gently eased the secret lid in the floor open, I held my breath, wondering what we were about to see.

And then I heard a voice behind us ordering me to stop what I was doing and step away.

As I pivoted around, I saw a familiar face holding a gun on us, and I knew that they'd been waiting all along for us to uncover the hidden treasure to claim it for themselves.

Chapter 21

"Very good," Carl Descent said as he looked greedily at the hidden cache we'd just uncovered. "What's inside the hole?"

"Sorry. It's empty," I said as I looked down, though what I'd told him was far from the truth. There were at least fifteen small velvet bags in the bottom of the opening, and each one looked as though it contained at least a dozen coins each. I had to stall Descent to give us time to come up with some way to counter his attack, and lying to him seemed to be the best option that we had at the moment. "How did you even know that anything was here?"

"I didn't, at least not with any degree of certainty," he said. "When your mother turned my final offer down today, I decided that I had to move quickly or risk losing the gold forever. My grandfather used to talk about it all of the time while he was still alive. It had been an obsession with him, and I caught the fever myself. I was about to break in when I saw you two coming, and from your expressions, I knew that you were on to something, so all that I had to do was to sit back and wait."

"Is that why you killed Sully?" I asked. "For the gold?" It didn't seem like any motive worth murdering someone over, at least not as far as I was concerned.

"He caught me snooping around, and he threatened to have me arrested for trespassing. I couldn't have that; someone might figure out what I was really doing here. When I tried to offer him a bribe to keep his mouth shut about finding me there, he got so angry that he grabbed me. The man was full of some brand of righteous indignation that I'd never seen before. What choice did I have? I had a right to defend myself, so that's what I did."

He'd found a way to justify the murder in his own mind, and I had to wonder if he actually believed what he was saying now. "And then you ran away."

"I did what I had to do," he repeated, almost like a mantra.
"It's still murder," I said.

Descent shrugged his shoulders. "Are you sure that it's in your best interest to convince me of that? If it's true, then what will a few more bodies matter in the end?" He gestured with his gun before he added, "Stop lying to me, Suzanne. I saw your eyes light up when you looked down. That cache isn't empty, is it?"

"Sorry. You're out of luck. I guess you killed Sully for nothing," Phillip said beside me. Good. I was thrilled that he was playing along. Maybe we'd make it out of this alive after all.

"I don't believe either one of you," he said as he gestured with his gun. "I'm not sure why I bothered asking; it will be easier for me to check after you're both dead. Now, I'm going to ask you one last time. What did you find?"

"There are bags of something down there, but I can't swear what they are. You should check it out for yourself," I said. If I could get him close enough, we might just have a chance to overpower him.

"You don't need that gun," Phillip said beside me. "We aren't going to resist. If it's indeed gold, take it. We won't try to stop you."

Descent seemed to be thinking about his options, and then finally he nodded in my direction, gesturing with his eyes that I was to follow his lead. I didn't know what he had in mind, but I suddenly had a plan of my own. However, much of it depended on what Descent did next.

"Why don't I believe either one of you? Go on. Reach in slowly and retrieve one of the bags." As Phillip started to comply with the order, Descent barked out, "Not you! Suzanne, you do it."

"I'm doing it," I said, making my voice quiver a little with fear. I didn't even have to fake it; I truly was frightened that we weren't going to get out of this alive. It was time to act, and fast.

We might not get a second chance.

I reached down and grabbed two bags, not one, as I'd been instructed. It felt as though there were plenty of coins inside when I lifted them; the bags were heavy, weighing more than they should have if they'd held anything but the precious metal Carl Descent had been dreaming about since he'd been a boy. It appeared that the small bags really did contain gold coins. I did my best to disguise the fact that I now held two bags, not one.

"Very good. You're doing fine. Now don't try anything tricky and toss it to me," Descent ordered, the avarice clear in his voice and his gaze.

This was going to be tricky. I had to toss one bag while still holding onto the other, all without the killer noticing. There was only one way I could do that. I had to spill one of the bags. Fortunately, the material had rotted sitting in that enclosure for all of those years, so one of the bags tore easily as I tugged on it.

"I'm waiting!" Descent said impatiently.

I didn't have any way of warning Phillip of what I was about to do, but that couldn't be helped. I just hoped that he didn't get shot in the process. Not only did I want him to stay safe, but I had no idea how I'd tell Momma if I somehow managed to get her husband shot.

As I tossed one of the bags to him, I made sure to spin it in the air in a high arc, and sure enough, gold coins tumbled out of the bag on the way down and scattered across the floor.

Descent was suddenly mad with lust for the gold now. He seemed to forget all about us for a moment as he dove for one of the rolling pieces, still shiny and bright after all those years.

It was the only chance we had. Taking the other bag in my hand, I swung it at his hand when he got close enough, doing my best to knock the gun out of his grasp.

I failed.

Carl Descent managed to step back out of my swing's arc, and the next thing I knew, Phillip was charging him full steam, and head on. The gun in Descent's hand exploded once, and I saw my stepfather jerk backwards with the impact of the bullet.

He'd been hit.

Without thinking, I launched myself at the killer. Descent was stronger than I was, but he wasn't expecting an all-out attack. I managed to knock the gun out of his hand, but I couldn't quite get control of it. As we both dove for the weapon, I knew that I had to stop him, or I'd join Phillip in his fate.

I wasn't even thinking as I drove my thumbs into his eyes, hoping to blind him with the fury for what he'd done raging through me.

He suddenly forgot all about the gun and started fighting me off, breaking my grip before I could do any substantial damage to his vision.

As his hands found the gun again, I knew that I was probably going to die.

And then, just as he started to lift the weapon to eliminate me as well, Phillip roared and dove onto him! He wasn't dead! As Descent went down in a heap, I joined Phillip on top of him, and the two of us finally managed to contain him when the former police chief finally managed to gain control of the handgun.

"Are you okay?" I asked him breathlessly as we both stood.

"Besides being shot, you mean? I'm just peachy," he said as he grimaced a little. "Luckily he caught me in the fleshy part of my upper arm. I'll be healed up in no time, but it's still no picnic. Take your phone out and call the police chief."

"There's no need to do that. I'm already here," Chief Grant said as he stepped out of the shadows. "Griffin saw you two going in, and then he watched Descent follow you. He called me, and here I am. Sorry I didn't get here any sooner, but it looks as though you two managed just fine without us."

"I didn't think you were watching the building anymore," I said as the police chief called for an ambulance for his former boss. Phillip handed the gun over to the acting chief and applied a handkerchief to his wound until the paramedics could arrive.

"I wasn't planning on anyone doing it," Chief Grant said, "at least not officially."

Officer Griffin explained as he joined us, "I had a hunch that something was about to happen here, so I decided to hang around some on my own time."

"And you spent your time off here, looking out for us?" I asked. "Don't get me wrong; I'm more grateful than I can say. Thank you." As Griffin pulled Descent to his feet and handcuffed him, I turned to my stepfather. "How bad is it, really?"

"Relax, Suzanne, it's no big deal. He just nicked my arm," the chief said as he continued to apply pressure to the wound.

"It looked much worse than that at the time," I said.

The chief grinned at me. "That's what I wanted him to think, too. That way he wasn't prepared when I jumped him a few seconds later."

"Thanks for doing that, by the way," I said.

"Hey, it wouldn't have worked at all if you hadn't spilled those coins on purpose and then went after him yourself. It turns out that we make a pretty good team."

"You know what? I think you're right," I said with a smile as the ambulance arrived. My stepfather was whisked away to the hospital, and Descent was led to the waiting squad car before I even realized what was happening. As everyone started to leave the scene, Jake burst in and wrapped me up in his arms.

"Suzanne, are you okay?" he asked breathlessly. "I just heard what happened."

"I'm fine," I said. "Phillip got shot, but it doesn't look that serious."

Jake frowned. "I don't have to remind you that I've been shot myself, and I can tell you from personal experience that it's never not serious."

"It was a through-and-through in the fleshy part of his arm," Chief Grant said. "All in all, if you have to get shot, it's a pretty good place for it to happen."

"I'm still not clear on what went down," Jake told me.

"Start from the beginning, and don't leave anything out."

"I wouldn't mind hearing the details myself," Chief Grant said.

"Fine," I said, and I retold my story to both of them, a performance that I'd repeat several times over the next few days. After I was finished telling them what had happened the first time, I looked at the coins on the floor and asked, "Shouldn't someone pick those up?"

"We need to get some photos first," the chief said. He whistled as he looked into the cache Phillip and I had found. "There appears to be quite a bit of gold down there. So, the rumors were true after all."

"It looks that way," I said. "I still can't believe Carl Descent would kill just to get his hands on some shiny gold coins."

"Do you have any idea how much it's probably worth?" the chief asked me. "People have killed for a lot less."

"I realize that, but I don't have to understand the motivation." I took Jake's hand. "We'd better get going. Momma is going to need us at the hospital for moral support."

"Let's go," he said as more police officers started to show up on the scene. "Can I do anything to help you here?" he asked Chief Grant before we left.

"No, I've got it covered." He paused, and then he added to me, "I'm glad you're okay, Suzanne."

"That makes two of us," I said with a grin.

As we drove to the hospital, Jake said, "You realize, don't you, that I'm never letting you out of my sight again."

"That's not very realistic, is it?" I asked. "Is there a chance you're overreacting?"

"Suzanne, I could have lost you today. Is that overreacting?"

"No," I said, "I think that's exactly the right amount of

reacting. It's going to be fine, though."

"Just don't go looking for any more hidden gold without me, okay?"

I grinned at him. "I can promise you that. What do you think Momma's going to do with her new fortune?"

"Your guess is as good as mine," he said as he drove. "I'm just glad that you're okay."

"So am I," I said.

As Jake pulled into the emergency room parking lot, I realized that I had everything in the world I needed, and no amount of gold or any other kind of material wealth would make the slightest bit of difference in my life. After all, I was richer than I had any right to ever expect, with a career I loved, a man to share my life with, and a community of family and friends that meant the world to me.

And in the end, what more could anyone ever ask for?

Chapter 22

"Jake, do you have a second?" Chief Grant asked him a little later as we waited in the hospital emergency room for them to patch Phillip up. Momma was back with him, pulling strings somehow to make sure that she saw every step they were taking to fix him, and we were waiting patiently for them to join us.

"What's up?"

"We need to speak with you," the acting chief said.

Jake looked around and grinned. "Is that the royal *we* you're using, or do you have some imaginary friends hiding behind you?" He was giddy from the relief that nothing had happened to me, and I enjoyed his silly side, mainly because I knew how fleeting it would be.

"I'm here," Mayor George Morris said breathlessly as he joined us. "How are you doing, Suzanne?"

"I'm as good as gold," I said with a grin. "How about yourself?"

"Ask me again in ten minutes. Jake?"

"I'll be right back," he said, and then he kissed me before he walked away with George and Chief Grant.

I couldn't help wondering what they were up to, but I knew that I'd find out soon enough. Jake and I didn't keep any secrets from each other, a rule I'd insisted upon after sharing my life with ex-husband Max the first time around.

I didn't have to wait by myself, though.

Grace showed up less than thirty seconds later. As I stood, she hugged me so tightly that I had trouble struggling for my breath. "Easy, pal. I'm okay."

"I had to see for myself when Stephen called me. Are you really all right?"

"Aside from a few scrapes and a bruise or two, I'm just dandy. You didn't have to rush over here on my account."

"That's where you're wrong," she said as she finally

released me. "Suzanne, I was wrong."

"About what?" I asked, not making the connection yet.

"I should have been there with you this evening, not Phillip."

I took her hands in mine and looked into her eyes. "Grace, it was exactly what you wanted to avoid. A killer was holding a gun on me, and it could have just as easily turned out to be tragic. You were right to take yourself out of the line of fire, and I respect your decision."

"Well, I don't," she said. "If something had happened to you, I never would have been able to forgive myself."

"What makes you think the outcome would have been any different?" I asked her. I wasn't trying to be mean, but she'd reached her earlier decision for a very good reason, and nothing had changed to impact that.

"If you're going to get yourself killed, I plan to be right there beside you from now on," she said. In a more timid voice, she asked, "If you'll have me, that is. Can I come back to the team?"

"Are you absolutely certain that's what you want to do?"

"I am, one hundred percent. Do you want to know the truth? I missed being in the middle of things. It turns out that my life is kind of predictable when I take you, and our investigations, out of the equation."

"I don't want to push you, but if you're sure, then I'd love to have you by my side again. Hopefully it won't come up for a long time, or maybe even forever."

"Well, if it does, I want to be in on it from the start with you." She stopped, looked over my shoulder, and then she added, "Why does Jake look as though he's the one who just got shot and not Chief Martin?"

I turned around to see what she was talking about, and sure enough, Jake looked stunned as he rejoined me.

"Hey, Grace. Suzanne, do you have a second? We need to talk."

"Why don't I like the sound of that?" I asked him. "Grace, whatever he has to say to me, he can say it in front of you."

"That's okay. Stephen's motioning for me to join him."
She hugged me once more before she left. "Thanks."
"It's my pleasure," I said. After she was ten steps away
from us, I asked Jake, "What's going on?"
"Something's come up, and I need your advice before I
make my decision," he said solemnly.
"I'm listening."
"Stephen Grant feels as though he's in over his head as
acting chief of police, and the mayor has asked me to step in
and take over until he's ready to assume the job on a full-
time basis."
"I thought you were finished with law enforcement," I said
in my most level manner.
"I thought so, too, but working this murder case with you
told me that I wasn't quite done with it yet. Would it be too
terrible if I took over for a year or two until Grant is ready to
assume the position permanently? He'll be my deputy chief,
and I'll have him ready to go by the time I'm ready to hand
the department over to him. If you don't want me to do this,
just say so, and I'll tell them that I'm not interested."
I took his hands in mine. "Jake, the only thing that matters
to me is that you're happy, so the real question is, would you
be happier being idle, or working at something you love
doing?"
He grinned at me. "When you put it that way, there's
really not much of a decision to make, is there?"
"Not in my mind, Chief," I said with a grin. "Look on the
bright side. You get to go back into law enforcement and
still sleep in your own bed every night. It's a win/win in my
book."
He kissed me soundly before he said another word.
"Marrying you was the best decision I ever made in my life,
bar none."
"Right back at you," I said. "Now go tell them the good
news."
"Thanks," he said, with more joy and enthusiasm than I'd
seen in him since he'd quit the state police. He'd been

getting restless, and this would make the perfect transition for him. I doubted that it would be his forever job, but it was exactly what he needed right now.

And I wouldn't have to retire my own amateur sleuthing either, now that Grace was back on board.

Maybe I'd even have more success, now that I was so close to someone on the inside.

One way or the other, we'd have to find some middle ground between Jake's new job and my penchant for investigation, but I had faith in us.

After all, no matter what, we would find a way to make it work.

RECIPES

A SIMPLE LEMON GLAZE

In two of the recipes below, I like to use a simple lemon glaze to ice the donuts when they're finished. Adding a little fresh lemon juice and zest to the glaze makes the donuts really pop. Truth be told, when I'm in the mood for the taste of lemon, this goes on just about anything I'm making at the time, including Belgian waffles! The recipe couldn't be simpler, so don't be afraid to try this one at home!

Ingredients
1 cup sifted powdered confectioner's sugar
1 to 2 tablespoons fresh lemon juice
1 teaspoon grated lemon zest

Directions
In a medium-sized bowl, mix the confectioner's sugar, lemon juice, and lemon zest, stirring well until you have the consistency you desire.
Use immediately, pouring the glaze over any donuts or other bready treats you happen to have handy.

Glaze will cover 1-2 dozen donuts, depending on how heavily you apply it

MOMMA'S HOMEMADE CHICKEN SOUP

This soup recipe is not just for when someone gets sick in my family, it's also perfect on a cool day in spring, summer, or autumn. We love the soup alongside a grilled cheese sandwich made with hot and gooey sharp cheddar cheese! This recipe has been tweaked over the years until it's near perfection, at least in our opinions. I give you my word that once you taste this soup, you'll never go back to anything that comes in a can!

Ingredients
1-2 cups cooked chicken, cut, diced, or chopped
4-6 ounces pasta, cooked (we like spaghetti noodles, but wide egg noodles work great, too)
4 cups chicken broth
2 carrots, peeled and chopped
1 tablespoon extra virgin olive oil
1 teaspoon chopped basil

Directions
In a large pot, heat the olive oil on a medium setting. While that is warming, in another smaller pot cook the pasta according to the directions on the package until it is al dente. Add the chopped carrots to the olive oil, sautéing until the carrots begin to soften. Next, add the broth, the cut-up chicken, and the basil, and simmer for ten minutes. Once the pasta is finished, add it to the simmering mixture and take off the heat immediately. Salt and pepper to taste, and enjoy.

Makes four servings

LEMON CRUSH DONUTS

In my household, lemon is always in fashion. There's something about the taste of it when it's mixed into a donut recipe that makes the treats spring to life for us. When we make these donuts, freshly squeezed and grated lemon is a real must. I love the smell as I grate a little of the peel for this recipe, and sometimes I simmer the leftover pulp in some water on the stovetop to infuse the kitchen with those zesty aromas. These donuts aren't exactly gorgeous, but they are tasty, so what's not to like? As I've said before, in my home, there are five things that count about the food we serve here: taste, taste, taste, taste, and appearance. The trick? Number five doesn't count!

Ingredients
Dry
1 cup flour, unbleached all purpose
1 teaspoon, baking powder
1/4 teaspoon lemon peel, grated
1 dash salt

Wet
1/2 cup whole milk
1/3 cup granulated sugar
4 tablespoons butter, melted
1 egg, beaten
2 teaspoons lemon juice, freshly squeezed
1/2 vanilla bean, scraped

Directions
In a bowl, mix the flour, baking powder, lemon peel, and salt until it is all thoroughly incorporated. In another bowl, mix

the whole milk, sugar, butter, egg, lemon juice, and the vanilla bean seeds together. Mix well, and then slowly add the dry ingredients into the wet until they are combined, being careful not to over-mix, as this could cause denser donuts.

Bake these donuts in a 375°F oven or in your donut maker for 6-8 minutes, then remove them to a cooling rack. You can make a simple lemon glaze using melted sugar, lemon juice, and a little grated lemon peel, or dust them immediately with powdered confectioners' sugar.

Yields 8-10 donuts.

ANOTHER QUICK DONUT MIX, THIS ONE WITH LEMON

I don't always feel like making a regular donut mix when I'm in a hurry for a quick treat, so I love to experiment with augmenting mixes that come prepackaged. One thing I've done lately is grab a lemon cake mix off the shelf of my pantry and convert the ingredients into some excellent donut batter. This recipe can be baked or deep-fried, depending on the final consistency you like your batter. For a more cake-like texture, just reduce the amount of milk you use. A great deal of this is accomplished playing it by ear, something I know many folks are afraid to do when they're baking. I say throw caution to the wind and have some fun. The worst thing that happens is your creation is a complete and utter failure, something that has happened to me in the past more times than I can count.
At the very least, you'll get a funny story out of it!

INGREDIENTS
Approximately 16 ounces of a lemon cake mix (we like Krusteaz lemon pound cake mix, but any mix is worth trying)
3/4 cup whole milk
10 tablespoons butter, melted
2 tablespoons freshly squeezed lemon juice
1 tablespoon grated lemon peel

DIRECTIONS
In a large mixing bowl, combine the cake mix, the milk, melted butter, lemon juice, and grated lemon peel, mixing until moistened.

Bake these donuts in a 375°F oven or in your donut maker for 6-8 minutes, then remove them to a cooling rack. You can make a simple lemon glaze using melted sugar, lemon juice, and a little grated lemon peel, or dust them immediately with powdered confectioners' sugar.

Makes 5-9 donuts, depending on baking method.

If you enjoy Jessica Beck Mysteries and you would like to be notified when the next book is being released, please send your email address to newreleases@jessicabeckmysteries.net. Your email address will not be shared, sold, bartered, traded, broadcast, or disclosed in any way. There will be no spam from us, just a friendly reminder when the latest book is being released.

Also, be sure to visit our website at jessicabeckmysteries.net for valuable information about Jessica's books.

Made in the USA
Middletown, DE
03 September 2015